Stilettos Can Be Murder

Stilettos Can Be Murder

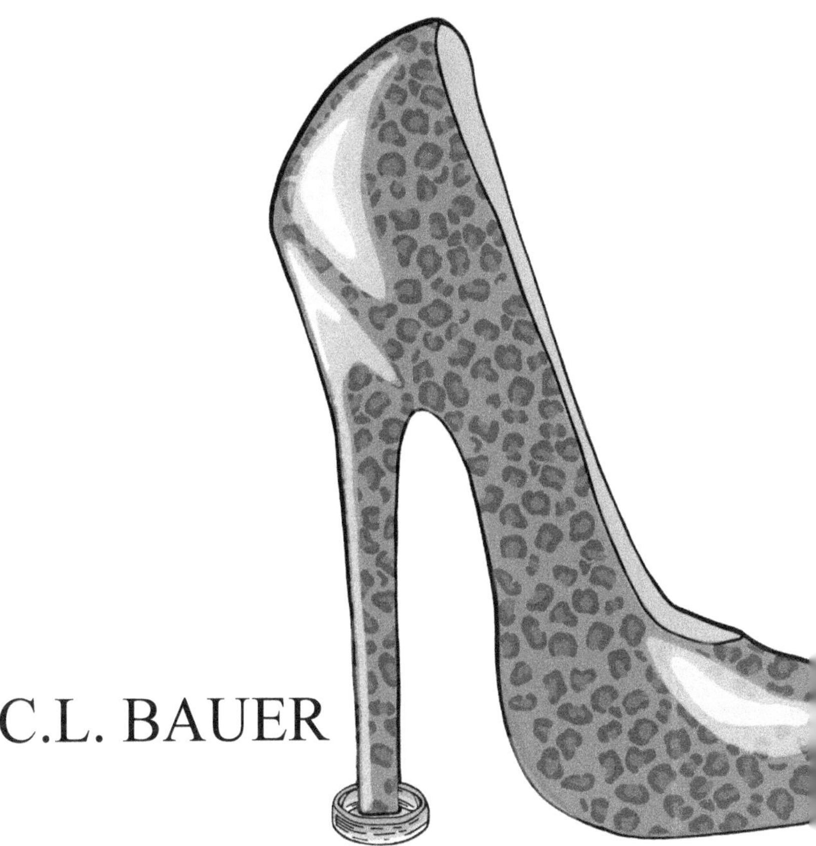

C.L. BAUER

For information contact:

www.clbauer.com

Cover Art By: Carolyn Schneck
Design: Miller Publishing LLC

ISBN: 978-1-7363460-4-4

First Edition: March 2021

10 9 8 7 6 5 4 3 2

The Lily List Mystery Series

The Poppy Drop
The Hibiscus Heist
The Tulip Terror
The Sweet Pea Secret

The Lily List Mystery Exclusives

Stilettos Can Be Murder

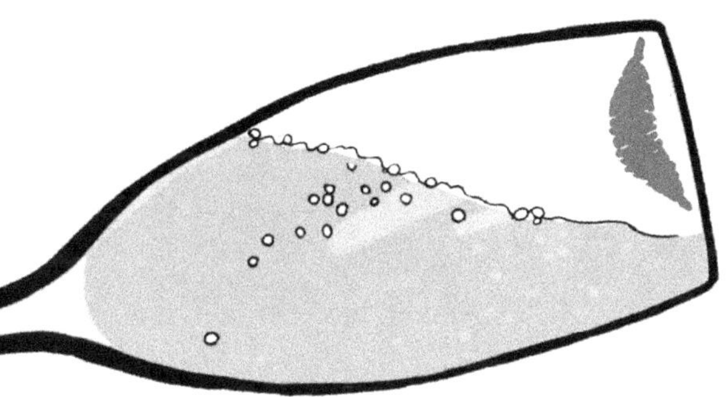

Dedication

Without our family's wedding flower business, I wouldn't know characters like Gretchen. Actual characters, people we know and love, make the world brighter and fuller. Always search for those loud individuals. There is always a story there. This book is for those over-the-top, in-your-face human beings who challenge you and love you when you least expect it.

Bless their hearts!

Chapter One

"I, Gretchen Malloy, being of sound mind, do hereby--" Gretchen stopped and peered over her cheetah print readers. "Really, Jameson? A will actually has this wording? Why can't we begin with I, Gretchen Malloy, being totally fabulous, and now you all are going to miss me? I hate a formal, stuffy document, don't you?"

Jameson Palmer inherited the formidable Ms. Malloy from his father. He didn't win her in a poker game, he lost to his brother. They threw dice, and the loser received Gretchen as his client. He hadn't realized that some of the ramifications of his father's retirement would totally ruin his life. Well, not totally, but enough to ruin a fine June afternoon. He wanted to be on the eighth hole instead of placating an aging socialite who knew every big client in his father's files.

"Ms. Malloy, we have to use that wording. A will contains your last requests before you leave this world." Jameson smiled in an attempt to appease the fifty-something, at least he thought she was, successful event planner. "When you die--"

Gretchen glared over her glasses now teetering on the edge of her nose. "**If**, if I die, young man. I plan on making a pact with the devil and coordinating every one of your children's weddings."

Jameson coughed uncontrollably. He'd just finally placed an engagement ring on his college sweetheart's finger. He didn't need to think about children yet, or their weddings. He hadn't had his own!

"Ms. Malloy, it is a wise decision to go ahead and have these things planned out just in case." He figured Gretchen had a hidden box containing her real beating heart. As long as no one discovered it or what it contained, she lived forever. He snickered quietly at his own joke.

"Excuse me? There's nothing funny about this. Besides, Mr. Palmer, you haven't made the wisest choices all of your life."

The young lawyer sat a little straighter in his chair and the smirk on his lips vanished.

Gretchen's gaze caught his. She held his focus. She watched as he became serious, tugging uncomfortably at his tie as though it was a noose. *Ah, I have him! What a little ninny. He's nothing like his old man.* "I remember when you couldn't keep your trunks on at Daria Peyton's swim party. You had just passed the bar." Gretchen's eyes narrowed. She leaned in across the table as though she had a secret to tell. "I have photos, young Palmer."

The attorney's jaw clenched. "Please read the rest to see if we need to make any changes." He wanted to call his father as soon as possible and ask him what on earth he had ever done to him to deserve Gretchen Malloy. Then he would call his brother and accuse him of using loaded dice.

He watched her as she slid her glasses further back on her nose and sat back in the chair. He watched her read every line. Frequently, she nodded. Jameson remembered the woman. Of course, she was older now. He'd have to look in her file to see if she really was in her fifties, but her hands looked the age. His mother always told him you could see someone's true age in their hands, and if they worked in an office or in the dirt. Here was a woman who never wallowed in self-pity or in a mud pile.

Jameson had memories of a New Year's Eve party years ago at his parents' home. He and his brother snuck down the stairs to watch the clock tick down to the new year. Gretchen had arrived near the stroke of midnight. She flew in as though she was on a comet, her bright streamers cutting through the dark sky. There was a roar of welcome. When she removed her full-length fur coat, there was a golden hue about her. She wore the shortest gold beaded dress. He had just turned thirteen, and he noticed the longest legs he'd ever seen. From then on, a woman with great legs drew his attention. On her feet, she wore the highest heels. She was the most beautiful woman he'd ever seen.

As Gretchen continued to read, he nonchalantly observed her footwear. Yes, she had on stilettos. His eyes trailed up from her ankles. She still had those lovely legs. Back then, he'd been a hormonal teenager. He was surprised that even now, he felt a pang of unbridled lust toward the woman across from him. She was saying something to him.

"Jameson, my executor's name should be Lily Schmidt Pierce, not just Mrs. Lily Pierce. She had a life before she married. You don't lose who you are just because you marry."

The attorney jotted down the change. "Is she a niece or distant relative? I've been meaning to ask, oh, and I'll need her contact information for the file."

Gretchen smiled softly. "She's my friend. She used to own the flower shop on the boulevard down from your parents' home. In fact, that little shop provided their wedding flowers. I'll get you her phone and address."

"Is she here in Kansas City?"

Gretchen's smile faded. *I wish.* "No, she's married and lives in Virginia. If I die, she'll have an excuse to come back home."

And what about your assets? You won't need to list them, will you?"

Gretchen frowned. She tried not to crease her skin; that action did leave permanent marks. "Excuse me? Have you met me? Jameson, let me enlighten you. I can buy and sell most of the people in this city. I don't flash my wealth. I retain it for a rainy day. Luckily, my life is usually sunny. I buy nice things, actually, only the best, but I don't need a lot to live my fullest life. Have you not learned anything from your father?"

Jameson thought he had been educated, but he was receiving an education from a different syllabus today. He felt as though he'd been taken out and spanked. He remained silent until she cooled down.

But Gretchen wasn't finished with him. "Don't you realize that people aren't always what they seem? Yes, I like my jewelry." Gretchen proudly displayed her right arm toward him. Adorned on her wrist was an expensive watch, a diamond bracelet, and another gold bracelet that featured a small heart dangling. "Some people are all show. Don't ever assume that someone has money from what they wear and how expensive the car is that they drive. They could have a lot of debt. I, on the other hand, only spend money on myself. Besides, I'm not flashy. I'm a very reserved woman."

Jameson bit his tongue so he didn't laugh. He remembered that party all those years ago because she had been the brightest bulb, the shiniest bauble. She swept into his parents' living room, and all he saw was a flash of gold. She was a living doll back then.

"Okay," he said softly. "All I really wanted to know is if you have anyone you'd like to designate your worldly possessions, your money, your car, and your apartment to such as family--"

Gretchen's head bowed in surrender. "I have no one." The silence in the room made her feel worse than how she was feeling as she had to face her own death. Death was inevitable, but she didn't have to like it, nor did she dwell on the inevitability of the subject. Death had taken away so many whom she had loved.

The young man's view of her softened. He saw a glimpse of that doll he'd fallen in love with as a teenager. Somehow, he knew if he pitied her he would pay dearly for it. She didn't want his pity; she just wanted his expertise.

"Ms. Malloy, you really don't have anyone? Do you spend money on anyone but yourself? Perhaps there's a charity you donate to that would be worthy of your financial attention."

Finally, Gretchen's eyes met his. He was rewarded with a smile. "Actually, I have some individual items I'd like to leave to Lily and to my other friend, Abby. I'll email that list to you, but I'd like to leave the majority of my estate to Lily's little man and any of her future children. They are my family. For now, there's just Andrew, but I'm sure they'll have other children. Lily owes me a little girl, and I can't believe the woman wouldn't want an excuse to spend time with her delicious husband."

Jameson found himself nodding. A woman owed her a child? His head was reeling from Gretchen Malloy's logic. He didn't want to ask about the delicious husband, but he did wonder how one received that description. "Of course. I'll make those changes, and just email me the other information. I can have this ready for you Saturday. Could you come in around ten?"

Gretchen placed the papers on his desk and stood up quickly. "What are you thinking? When did your brother get married?"

Jameson was perplexed. "It was last April. I don't remember the day."

What day of the week was it, Jameson?" Gretchen crossed her arms. She tapped her foot on the hardwood floor.

The attorney gulped. "It was a Saturday."

"Exactly." Gretchen threw back her hair. "I am working this Saturday on the Hampton wedding. I can't be fooling around with my will on the day of one of the biggest events in the city. My work always comes first, as should yours. I can come by Monday, say one in the afternoon?"

Jameson viewed his phone's calendar. Gretchen did the same. "That will work. I'll have it ready on Monday. Thank you, Ms. Malloy."

His client flung her designer bag over her arm. Before

she reached the door, she turned back around. "Jameson, please offer your parents my regards, and if you're going to check out someone's legs under the desk, make sure you do it without them noticing."

Gretchen left a red-faced young attorney in her wake. She smiled as she closed the door behind her and waved at the two paralegals in the outer office. As she reached her car, she laughed out loud.

"You've still got it, Gretchen. You're not dead yet!"

Chapter Two

Another Saturday, another wedding. Any wedding coordinator and planner worth their salt and price was working this first weekend of June. If you weren't, you were absolutely nothing in the wedding industry. June was the go-to month. In Kansas City, it was **the** month, at least that's what Gretchen Malloy thought. Of course, October was **the** month too, but June brides wanted to be June brides. When you said, "October Bride" it just didn't have the same romantic ring to it. Gretchen Malloy thought quite a bit about many things. She had an opinion about everything and everyone. Luckily, her opinions were always correct, even when others might think they were wrong. She was harsh only when someone needed a dose of reality. That happened quite frequently.

Gretchen was the best and most expensive coordinator in the metropolitan area. She planned and organized just about every socially important occasion over the last thirty years. To some she was the ultimate party planner, rivaling famous divas who performed the same work. To others, she was a large pain in the arse.

At today's wedding, she was there to oversee all of the wedding workings of the day and to make sure no cog was stuck or broken in the process. Gretchen peered down at her gold Rolex watch.

Darn it. I can't see," she whispered. Her vanity was

surely getting the best of her. She had her newest pair of glasses in her bag. They were the most divine shade of purple with flecks of gold around the rims. Although they were the cutest readers, the eyewear would remain hidden in the bag today. She had the feeling that the bride already considered her a dinosaur. She didn't dare give the girl ammunition by wearing an outward reminder of an inner feeling. She felt old today, almost ancient. Perhaps writing up a will wasn't the most prudent idea after all. But, she did understand first hand that life was fleeting, and for some, they would never have the opportunity to fly. She shook off the thought and squinted again. Now she could see that there were only thirty minutes remaining before the wedding ceremony was scheduled to begin.

Guests were filling the lobby of the massive church. There were hugs and kisses all around with reunions among long-missed relatives. Gretchen shifted her weight on her four-inch stilettos. Maybe she was getting too old, at least too old to wear these heels all day. Her love affair with high heels of any kind began when she read a magazine article in high school. The article changed her life--the higher the heel, the longer your leg looked. It was a simple theory of addition and subtraction with amazing results. Most people changed their lives with education or love, but for Gretchen it was that one bit of style sense that transformed her life and became her fashion signature.

Her left calf muscle of her long lean legs was cramping. Perhaps the two varicose veins she'd sighted the other day were creating the chaos? All aging processes needed to stop immediately. Later tonight she could slowly lower her weary body into a nice bath, surrounded by quiet, bubbles, and with a wine glass in her hand. Then, and only then, in the privacy of her bath would she allow herself to wallow in ageism and self-pity. Only then, when no one could see. She had a reputation to maintain.

"Gretchen, have you seen the groom or groomsmen? I think I saw the groom when he first arrived, but that was almost an hour ago," the wedding photographer, Graham Patchett complained.

Gretchen pretended to see the time on her watch. "They should be taking photos with you. Perhaps you should have corralled them?" Her tone was as demeaning as it was intended.

"I've been taking photos of the bride and bridesmaids since I couldn't find the guys. Even the women were late. The bride ran some errand."

Gretchen knew this was going nowhere. "Fine. I'll go back and check on him. I just have this feeling our schedule will go to hell very soon." She glared at Graham as though he was the offender. He wasn't the usual photographer she preferred, but the bride and groom had selected him before Gretchen was hired as the coordinator. So here they were, less than thirty minutes before the wedding and no groomsmen or groom in sight.

Gretchen needed the shortest path possible. The brick and stone church covered in ivy had been built over six decades ago. Although it was conveniently located only three minutes from the reception venue, the older church didn't allow Gretchen an easy path. She quickly headed down the side aisle. The guests noticed her quickened steps, but it was her heels clicking on the slate floor that drew the most attention. She looked straight ahead, a woman on a mission. As she came to the room next to the sacristy, she noticed the heavy wooden door was closed. She leaned her ear to its frame and heard nothing. There was no laughter, no murmured words. Gretchen had discovered a phenomenon over the years that males of a wedding party were always louder than the women. *What is going on with this group? They've been unusual the last few days.*

"Trent? It's Gretchen. Are you in there? You better be in there." Still no answer. "Trent, I'm coming in. You boys better be dressed."

The wedding coordinator turned the knob and slowly opened the door. The groom was sprawled on the floor. He was completely alone. *At least he's dressed.* She shut the door with a shove, hoping the sound would wake him.

"Trent, this is ridiculous. You boys drank entirely too much last night. I warned you. By the way, where are your groomsmen?" Gretchen scanned the room. There wasn't any evidence that the group had even been there. Not one red solo cup or can of beer could be seen.

"Come on, Trent. Wake up." She gently placed the narrow tip of her shoe into his ribs. He didn't move one inch.

"I can't kneel down. Come on." She shoved harder with her shoe. Still the body remained rigid. *How can you not feel that?* There was no groaning. She directed one heel to the edge of his collar and pushed slightly. There was still no movement, but she noticed a liquid of some kind on her shoe from his neck. She couldn't see clearly enough to determine what it was.

"If this is vomit, there will be hell to pay. This isn't funny, Trent. I know your mother, and she won't be amused if you are too drunk to even stand in front of the altar. It will be the story of the city." Delicately, Gretchen stepped over his body to look down at his face. "Trent?"

Finally, she sighed. *I better be able to get back up again. My knees can't take this. My eyes aren't the only parts of my body failing me!* She crouched down beside him and saw two tiny blood marks on his neck. It appeared to be--Gretchen stopped and smiled. The marks looked like vampire bites, or--

"So there's a vampire roaming in the daylight of Kansas City?" She laughed at her own question. "This really isn't funny. Where's the camera, boys?" She looked around to discover the "gotcha" pranksters, but she saw no one.

She placed her finger down to look at the marks. There was very little blood. Now she realized what was on her shoe. Gretchen shoved the groom's arm. She reached for his wrist to feel a pulse. *Nothing. Nothing?* Gretchen Malloy, for the first time in many years, was speechless. In her shock, she lost her balance, falling backward onto her bottom.

"He's dead," she whispered. "The wedding is ruined." The gossip, and actual news of this, could ruin everyone's reputation. She was helpless to fix this situation. *Who am I kidding? This isn't a situation. I can't fix a death no matter how many connections I have in this city!* A groom is dead. She should call someone, but she really didn't want to believe that this was happening. *Maybe it's just a spasm? Maybe he's in some sort of coma?* The vampire scenario suddenly became a viable option.

Suddenly, the door opened, and Gretchen Malloy was seen next to a dead body. Framed in the open door well, stood the mother and father of the groom, Delbert and Rhonda. The Hamptons were an old Kansas City family, acquiring most of their money from Delbert Sr.'s construction and engineering company. Rhonda had been a Junior Leaguer and was on various charity boards around town, including one of the hospitals and for the major art museum. Gretchen and she had planned many of the fundraising events over the last ten years.

"What is going on?" Rhonda was shocked at the view before her. "What is Trent doing?"

"I found him this way," the usually composed woman stammered. "Rhonda, this isn't good."

"The boys are just pulling up. We were held up at the hotel. Just our luck that the party bus had a flat tire. Can you believe that? What company allows their vehicle to have a flat tire?"

Trent's father came closer to his son's body. "They can't help it, Rhonnie. I told you to let it go. We are here before the wedding begins. What is the boy doing? Has he passed out again? I warned him. He can't drink that much alcohol and expect his health not to suffer."

"There won't be a wedding," Gretchen said softly. "We need to call the police."

Delbert knelt down beside his son. "Stop joking, Trent. This is ridiculous. I know you weren't big on this whole wedding thing, but you made me a commitment. Now, get up."

Gretchen watched as the father patted his son and began to search his body. He saw the small marks on his neck. He moved the body slightly back and forth and realized what the coordinator already knew.

"Jesus," the father muttered. "Rhonda, get out of here." He was already reaching for his phone, dialing 9-1-1. "Yes, police, please come to St. Paul's. My son isn't responding. Please hurry. It's his wedding day."

Gretchen marveled at the man's composure. Her stomach was churning. She'd never had a groom die during one of her weddings. There was one time when a bride lost her life, but Gretchen put that aside. She couldn't think about that right now or she'd surely throw up what little breakfast she had eaten.

Rhonda Hampton obediently fled the room, leaving her husband and Gretchen alone with her son. The mother decided she'd go to the church lobby and greet guests. She put on her best smile; Delbert would handle everything. In fact, he always handled everything, even requiring a son to marry a certain young lady of a certain family. If Trent goofed up this wedding and this marriage, she would kill him.

Meanwhile, Trent Hampton's body remained stretched out on a cold wood floor. Gretchen couldn't move her legs. They had fallen asleep. Delbert Hampton continued to look over his son's body, touching here and there, and retrieving a paper or two from the groom's right pocket.

"We shouldn't move or remove anything," Gretchen suggested. She knew some police procedures thanks to a drug case she had been involved in a couple of years ago with her dear meddling Lily. Gretchen remembered that time fondly as the time they bonded. They became more than the passing coordinator and florist at a wedding. They became friends. Lily and she had investigated one of the best families of Kansas City discovering their participation in illegal activities. *Who would've imagined that the grandson and the son would be involved in the drug world? That was a good time!*

Delbert glared. "He is my son. I'll take whatever I want, and you won't say anything to anybody, Gretchen. You understand?"

Gretchen nodded, but she really didn't understand. She was deep in thought, wondering what he was all about when she heard the first siren. She would go out there and flag them down, but she still couldn't get up. After a minute of intense rubbing of her legs, she could feel them again. But it would be difficult to get up without touching the poor boy's body.

Delbert Hampton rose up and walked out into the parking lot to hail the ambulance, the fire department, and the police car that was pulling into the driveway. To Gretchen, it seemed like every siren in the city was heading their way.

Gretchen was stuck as man after man and one female paramedic flooded into the room. The woman smiled at her. "Can I help you up, ma'am?"

She hated *ma'am*, but she did appreciate the assistance. "I just need to walk around a bit. I've been down on that floor for a while."

The paramedic assisted her out of the room and stood next to her as more first responders flooded by them. The activity was frantic, as though they could save him.

One policeman exited the tight room and came over to her. "Ms. Malloy, were you the one in the room with the groom?"

She nodded.

"What were you doing there?"

"I'm the wedding coordinator. I was checking on him. It was thirty minutes before the wedding."

"I see. How long were you in there with him before it happened?"

Gretchen blinked. "Before what happened?" "Before his death." The police officer was looking down at her shoes.

Gretchen looked down at her feet and then up to face him. "He was dead when I arrived, well at least he was dead when I checked him."

"Could you please take off that right shoe?" He pointed down.

"And why would I do that?" Once Gretchen had asked, she noticed the very friendly paramedic release her arm and back away.

"Because I need that shoe."

"And I need it too. How am I supposed to walk without my shoe? What is your name?"

"My name is Officer Erickson. Give me that shoe or I will take it off of you." His tone had changed from determined to threatening. Gretchen didn't do well with bullies, nor condescending tones; she never had since high school.

Gretchen emitted a noise somewhere between irritation and outrage, but she leaned down and removed her left shoe and then the right one, handing it directly to the officer. "Are you happy?"

He didn't smile. He looked into her eyes and back to the stiletto. Gretchen followed his gaze. "How did you get this on your shoe?"

"Well, I guess when I touched him."

The police officer's blue eyes seared through her. "It appears to be blood. Did you use it to kill that young man?"

Gretchen saw her life flash by. *I had my first pony ride when I was five. My prom date was the banker's son. He brought the wrong-colored flowers for my corsage. My first car was a blue Ford Mustang. I stole a lipstick at the only department store in Peoria. I have had more than my share of speeding tickets, but I always had a reasonable alibi. Wait! What?* Gretchen left memory lane to return to the present.

"I didn't kill Trent Hampton. He was dead when I saw him in the room. I kicked him, and I pushed back his collar with my heel. That's when my shoe was spotted."

The officer continued to examine the shoe. "When you kicked him?"

"I thought he was passed out drunk. Last night, after the rehearsal, the groom and the groomsmen were a little out of control. The groom even made a pass at me, but he mentioned he had the wrong woman." *I probably shouldn't have said that!* That one sentence did indeed trigger a response. The officer's brows elevated at least an inch, and his lips formed one slim line. *I abhor a thin-lipped man. You can't trust them.*

"She was probably upset that he didn't want her," Delbert Hampton stated plainly as he approached the policeman. "She was all over him at the rehearsal party."

Gretchen clutched her heart in dramatic fashion. "What are you talking about? He is a boy. I don't play with clients." A young man was nice now and then, but Gretchen Malloy never toyed with a client. She had her standards.

"You have anything else to tell me, ma'am?"

Gretchen folded her arms in front of her ample chest. She glared at Mr. Hampton. "Get a warrant."

Officer Erickson shook his head. "Lady, you are in some serious trouble."

In what seemed a matter of minutes, Gretchen found herself sitting in the back of a police car that reeked from the stench of old smoke and unclean bodies. She watched the melodrama unfold in front of her as Rhonda was told of her son's death. Gretchen noticed the mother didn't cry, instead she looked in her direction and mouthed an obscenity. The woman was angry and full of fury, but she wasn't tearful. *That's interesting.* Gretchen shook it off quickly. She only had thoughts of upcoming events, including one she was planning at the end of the month with Rhonda. *I suppose I'll be without her help now.*

Gretchen's arms were turning red in the warm car. She really needed her bag. She needed to check her lipstick and dab at the tiny beads of sweat rolling down her forehead. She saw two men in suits heading her way; they had her bag and folders.

"Could I have my bag? I really need a touch-up on my lipstick," she yelled from the half-open window. One man laughed and the other shook his head.

They arrived in front of her. "This bag is evidence, and lady you don't need to be pretty where you are going."

"Excuse me? What is going on here? I know people."

One suited man leaned on the car to peer in at her like she was some caged animal. "You are in a lot of trouble, and you'll need to know the President to get you out of this mess."

Gretchen blinked her lavish lashes, her very fake lashes. "I did plan a party for him in Palm Beach once. If you give me my phone, I can call him."

The man's face contorted in disbelief and irritation. He opened his mouth to speak, then thought better of it. He began to walk away, taking only one step before he turned and leaned in. "Geez, lady, who are you?"

"I am Gretchen Malloy, and I'm the best event coordinator and planner in the city."

He turned his head to one side, looking similar to a small innocent puppy. "Ms. Malloy, we are taking you into custody. We'll be formally questioning you as a suspect in the murder of Trent Hampton."

Gretchen turned her eyes up to the roof of the car. She spotted a piece of dried gum and some other substance. "Does anyone ever clean this thing? Have you thought about a new color to lighten the interior? You'd see the dirt better." That was now the least of her problems.

Chapter Three

"Could I have a cup of coffee, please? It's cold in here, and I'm right under an air vent."

Gretchen glanced down at her cuffed hands. *My, this is a long way from those fur handcuffs with the lovely rhinestone at the lock in Beverly Hills years ago.* She smiled just remembering those cuffs, the man, and that one night. She still loved to watch his movies. It wasn't that he was a thespian of Brando's caliber. He was just nice to admire especially when he was wet and sauntering out of the ocean toward her.

She remembered fondly that one special night in those fur cuffs. Some cherished autographs, but Gretchen preferred memorable souvenirs, ones that still made you smile when they crossed your thoughts.

Police rushed by the desk where she was seated, but no one paid her any attention. She looked down at her watch. Her glasses were still in her bag, and the bag was in the chair across from her. She tried to get up a few minutes ago. That hadn't gone well when the entire room of people ignoring her suddenly gave her their every attention. They ran toward her as though she was a serial killer. She was not some criminal. But she was certainly being treated like one.

Finally, a very nice-looking man touched her on the shoulder. Gretchen looked up to see grey eyes. *Are those specks of gold? My, where has he been hiding himself? Oh, right, he's the one that said something to me while I was in the police car.* Unlike most men who were in Gretchen's age group, this one had a full head of hair with just touches of a few grey flairs at his temple. She figured he was in his forties, or he might be a well-preserved fifty something. "Ms. Malloy, we are ready now. Come with me."

Although she desperately wanted to flirt with him, the better part of valor would be to remain silent until spoken to. *I won't offer them one piece of information. They can do their jobs. Of course, I know absolutely nothing.* Gretchen was led into a quiet room, an interrogation room. She'd seen enough of these empty spaces on detective television shows to know what went on in them. Fortunately, or unfortunately she sat across from the nice face. Before he questioned her, she examined him. Not only did he have those cat-like eyes and a good head of hair, his face was tanned and featured a chiseled jaw. *He's ruggedly handsome. My, look at those tanned forearms. If he works out, it must be low impact. He had a nice chest, but those arms. Perhaps he was a baseball player? I love that sport, well really the men. My day would be made with this detective.* Gretchen's musings were stopped abruptly by a low voice, a very male voice.

"I'm Detective Williams, Ms. Malloy, and we need to question you about the murder of Trent Hampton. I hear you wanted a relationship with the young man, even though you were planning his wedding."

Gretchen's mouth flew open. "I wasn't planning his wedding, I was coordinating it. There is a great distinction. Have you not heard of me? I'm on television every spring talking about weddings, and I have countless articles where

I've been quoted about that event or wedding."

The detective heard her and shook his head. He looked down at the file in front of him. "But you wanted a relationship with him?"

"Are you crazy?" She laughed for the first time today. "The boy is not my type. His shoulders slope, and he is getting a little gut on him. I much prefer washboard abs." Her eyes lowered from the man's broad shoulders to his muscled chest. *You are much more my type. I'd allow him to use those handcuffs again.*

The file hit the table. "Do you think this is a joke?" Williams was not laughing. "You are in some serious trouble, ma'am. You wanted this young man, right?"

He used that ma'am word! "Absolutely not. He was a client, and he isn't my type. Well, he wasn't my type. I've told you that. Actually, you are more my type." Without thinking, she ran her tongue over her lips. He was lovely, but actually she was very thirsty. "Could I possibly have a cup of coffee? It's a little chilly in here. Does the mayor not like you? Is that why he keeps your offices as cold as a morgue?"

Williams ignored her comment of discomfort. "I believe someone is getting a coffee for you. So, Hampton was just a client to you?"

"Yes, of course. I never play with young men who are about to be married. I am a professional." Gretchen began to thump her well-manicured nails on the table. She was getting anxious and a bit worried.

The detective chuckled. "I'm attempting to discover what kind of a professional you are." He allowed his eyes to roam over her from head to waist. Her full hair seemed to be sprayed in place, framing her face to her shoulders. Obviously, she colored her hair. Her makeup was very upscale, but there were elements of incongruity. Her lashes were lavish, long, and fake. Her eye shadow was masterfully applied, but so heavy on her lid that creases were beginning to form, and her lipstick was too bright for an older lady like her. Her sleeveless brown dress hugged every inch of her ample bosom, tapering down to full curves. He was sure every man wanted her about thirty years ago.

Gretchen didn't appreciate the innuendo. She was not paid for sex, well she did accept gifts, and if someone wanted to send her a piece of jewelry that said *Gretchen* on it, she wasn't one to refuse a lovely memento of a night well spent. But she didn't appreciate the detective's tone. She began to say something, but another officer entered the room and placed a coffee in front of her.

She raised the much-anticipated liquid to her mouth and took a sip. It was hot. Its taste was bitter, perhaps the worst cup of coffee she had ever had. She wasn't even sure it was coffee, perhaps tar juice, if that was such a thing. She pursed her lips. In past years she rated the coffee during her travels. Obviously, Seattle's airport featured the richest flavor in the country. *But a Cuban espresso is good if you're in Miami.*

"This won't do," she admitted as she shoved the cup toward her opposing inquisitor. "I need a real coffee. Perhaps you could go down to the coffee shop a couple blocks down the way and pick me up a large caramel sunshine? If that's not available, the Kansas City brew is my favorite. That would give me a little pick-me-up."

"Do you need other things to give you a little pick-me-up?" The investigator wondered if Ms. Malloy was high or just naturally annoying. Her thought processes seemed disjointed. If this was her real persona, why did anyone hire her to do anything?

"What? No, I just need caffeine and a decent cup of coffee. Frankly, I don't like your implication." Gretchen drummed her nails louder on the table. She was tired. Even to her, the nails sounded similar to a woodpecker's pecking.

"I want you to go through the events while you were with the body." Gretchen could tell the detective was judging her, and not just for her involvement in a murder. He judged her guilty. He just met her. *At least most people take an hour before they judge me negatively.* They feared her professionally, or tired of her detailed phone calls, and incessant clicking of her high heels on a marble floor. There could always be a myriad of reasons why people didn't like Gretchen. She knew that, and most times she didn't care one bit what they thought. *This isn't one of those times.*

"I've already told you."

"Then humor me. Tell me again." Williams was realizing she wasn't impaired, just privileged.

Gretchen pulled back her hands. *I'm not getting a coffee, and now I'm hungry. Could I barter for food?*

"If I tell you everything, may I get something to eat?"

The detective sat a bit straighter with his sudden interest. He pulled his chair closer and leaned across. "Of course. You tell me everything, and I'll make sure you get a meal." He looked at his watch. His own stomach was growling as though it knew it was almost eight in the evening.

"Fine. I came in to check on Trent. The photographer wanted to take photos. I went back to see him. I came into the room and saw him on the floor. I kicked him. I nudged his collar. I came closer at some point, after I had walked over him. I saw two marks on his neck from a vampire, well what looked like fang marks. I fell back on my rump, and the groom's parents opened the door." She sighed as the very bland, delicious detective blinked a couple of times. "I would like a steak from Garnett's. It's in the Crossroads. I need it medium rare and served with their parsley potatoes, and a salad with a champagne vinaigrette. I'd also like their special flan. They usually garnish it with a fruit of some kind. I'd prefer strawberries."

Williams hit the table with both hands, the sound reverberating within the room. "Ms. Malloy," Detective Williams yelled. "I'm not a waitress."

Despite the man's fury frightening Gretchen to death, she pulled it together quickly for a response. "Server, you don't say waitress anymore, Detective Williams. Years ago, we women condemned the words waitress and secretary. We have broken through the glass ceiling, well at least we've chipped it. It'll crack soon. Women and men are equals in every way."

The man threw the file across the room. All sanity had departed. "We are holding you as a suspect in a murder. A murder, Ms. Malloy. You are in some big trouble. You're treating this as some inconvenience. A man is dead, and I believe you killed him."

Gretchen bit her lip. *I will not give him the satisfaction of seeing me cry. I never give any man that.* "I want my phone call. We still get those, don't we?" Thoughts of a steak and her favorite meal flew away with that file.

"I'll call whomever you want."

"No. I need my phone. All my contacts are on that phone."

"We can contact your lawyer."

"I don't want my lawyer, well he is a lawyer, but I need someone else if this is such a big deal."

The detective stood up. "A young man dead on his wedding day is a pretty big deal." He headed for the door and turned around. His suspect still sat staring at where he had been seated. "I'll grab your phone, but I'll be doing the calling." Between her haughtiness, her demands, and the brief lecture about equality and women's rights, he just wanted her out of his hair and in a cell somewhere boring other prisoners. He was breaking protocol for her, but it would give him an opportunity to look through the contacts on her phone. Besides, he couldn't wait to see who she brought in. Hopefully she didn't call someone who was a lawyer on some television program.

The detective reached inside the wedding coordinator's bag that was already enclosed in a rather large evidence packet. "Hey, all, each item in her bag needs to be tagged and bagged." No one was listening as they scurried about the room. He knew a designer bag when he saw one. His ex-wife used to fawn over these three initials on a piece of leather. It was just an overpriced piece of cow that left his wallet lighter, but to his former wife it had been everything that last Christmas. She loved anything that was the most expensive. For Ms. Malloy, it seemed her style was highly materialistic as well. In his search of the bag, he removed a brush, hairspray, dental floss, and two bags of makeup.

There was more including a pair of slippers and a zebra printed sleeping mask. Finally, he discovered the cell in the bottom of the bag.

The woman didn't have her phone password protected, so he took a peek at her contacts. He swiped. His eyes grew wide as he saw name after name--the president, the state's governor, a congressman, an NFL coach, another coach, several football players, an Oscar winner--the detective could make a mint leaking these numbers and addresses. He shook his head.

"She really does know some important people." The detective quickly returned to his suspect and stood inside the open door. "Ms. Malloy, who do you want me to call for you?"

Gretchen glared at him. "I'd like to talk directly to him, please." Her hands motioned for him to throw the phone.

"Tell me who I need to look up for you. I'll hold the phone for you," he said as he stood beside her.

"Fine," Gretchen spit out. "Please hit the number for Hal."

The detective did as he was instructed and placed the phone up to her ear.

"Hi, honey. It's Gretchen. Oh, fine. Well, not so fine. Oh, you've heard already? It was on the news? I was afraid of that. Did they name me? Oh, no. Well, that's why I'm calling you. I'm sitting at one of your police stations. Oh, good, you know where. Could you come down and get me out? I hate to impose on Miranda and you. Oh, thank you. Maybe you can talk to this nice Detective Williams.

No, I'm a suspect, or they find me suspicious. I find myself captivating, but that's on a normal day." Gretchen glanced back and smiled at the hovering man. "Wonderful. I'll see you in a few."

The detective pulled the cell away. Gretchen sighed. *Being arrested is exhausting.* "He'll be here soon. He'll want to know the charges and see all the evidence."

"Fine, Ms. Malloy. I'll be happy to talk to your lawyer, not your lawyer or even Hal the plumber. We'll just sit in here together until he comes."

"That's fine with me. Oh, he did say not to say anything more to you. Will that affect our relationship, detective?" Gretchen smiled sweetly and batted her eyelashes quickly as Williams sat across from her.

Surprisingly, he laughed, a dimple appearing on his chin. "We have no relationship, Ms. Malloy. Actually, silence would be a fantastic idea. I suggest you pray."

Gretchen smirked. "And I suggest you better have your ducks in a row by the time my friend gets here." *He may be handsome, but he needs a little lesson in humility.* She suspected a little manscaping wouldn't hurt either. He had beautiful nails, but he was in bad need of a manicure. *He acts confident, but he bites his nails. Hmm, what secrets do you have, detective.* Her eyes followed to his left hand's ring finger. There was no ring. *There's not even a tan line where there used to be one. I'll have to get to the bottom of that story. Besides, I'd love to see his hair a little mussed.*

Detective Williams looked down at the rhinestone encrusted cell phone and then up into the face of a woman he had thought was old enough to be his mother. On second and third look, she probably wasn't old enough to be his mother, but she held herself as though she was a siren from the golden era of Hollywood. She was beautiful in her own way. He couldn't figure her out, and he definitely wouldn't want to play poker with her; her bluffs would kill him. She was bluffing wasn't she?

Almost thirty minutes later and several requests for better coffee, Detective Williams saw the door open slowly. The mystery lawyer had arrived. Williams immediately stood up. His suspect looked around, relieved.

"You're Ms. Malloy's lawyer?" Williams asked incredulously. His mouth shut tight. The man before him wasn't a television attorney, nor was he just a lawyer.

Mayor Jacquard smiled at Gretchen. "Let's get you out of those cuffs."

Gretchen Malloy smiled, but one tiny, almost invisible tear rolled from her left eye. She took her first free breath of the day. "Hal, I am so relieved to see you."

"Detective, I've already talked to your superiors. I'm sure we can get Ms. Malloy out of here in the next few minutes. What do you think?"

Mayor Henry "Hal" Jacquard was formidable, not just because of his over six-foot frame. He exuded power and control from his face to his voice. His body had softened over the years, but his broad chest proved he still maintained his workout regiment. His knees betrayed him in his later years as a professional football player. He couldn't run, but he could still walk in some of the charity runs around town. After football, his resonating low voice was perfect for trial law and for politics. He was an advocate for a safe city and a friend of the police department. His dad had retired from the force.

"Sir, Ms. Malloy is a suspect." Detective Williams cleared his throat. "We have evidence."

"Of what?" Hal placed his hand on his friend's back to offer moral and physical support. He'd never seen Gretchen Malloy looking out of sorts; she seemed disheveled and drained from the long day. The normally in charge coordinator was rightly a fish out of water in a police station. "You don't even have the autopsy started, do you?"

"I believe it has begun."

"Well, then, until there is a determination of how that young man died, you have nothing to charge. So what that she was found with the body. Look, Gretchen helped us with our daughter's wedding last year, and she had to track down the groom and his buddies in a Westport bar. That's what she does. Now, what I do is vouch for my citizens. This one is not a flight risk. Until you charge her, she's leaving with me. She'll be at her home, and I'm sure you already have all that information."

Gretchen looked back at her savior. "I need my bag and phone back too. They have everything, and I need my files. I have some info for Marty's campaign announcement party in there."

"Oh," Hal murmured. "Yes, you will need that." Mayor Jacquard stared down the quiet detective. "Inventory, take your photos, do your swabs, whatever you need. We'll be waiting for her items."

Gretchen smiled. *The detective is quiet? How do you like it in the hot seat, Williams?*

"Ms. Malloy can get her things at my desk. Just this way." He left the room quickly, fleeing from the mayor.

"That didn't take long, now did it?" Hal held out a hand to assist Gretchen up from the chair.

"Have I told you I love you? I'd love you even more if you had a sandwich on you."

"No sandwich, dear, but we will get you something on the way home. Let's get you out of here."

Thanks to the Mayor of Kansas City, Gretchen Malloy was safely at home within an hour. She was also eating a salmon salad from a closed restaurant. Thanks to Hal, the restaurant opened its locked door--Hal knocked loudly and the workers recognized him--and Gretchen had her first sustenance since breakfast. Under her dining room table, her feet had escaped the captivity of her slippers and were enjoying the softness of the carpet. Proudly, she wore her slippers out of the station. Her heels were remaining in custody. She sat alone, in the silence of her sanctuary. *So that's what the big house is like?* In her Christmas letter she would have to detail how she survived prison, well only for a few hours, and she wasn't ever jailed, but she was formulating some helpful hints for the common man.

She relished every bite of lettuce, salmon, and the slice of bread. It wasn't the freshest bread, but this time she would forgive the chef. Her wine glass was full, but soon it would be drained. She rested the bottle next to her glass so she wouldn't have to move one inch. Gretchen closed her eyes. She saw the groom's body on the floor. She saw the puncture marks on his neck. She heard the accusations from the groom's father. He had thought she wanted the young man.

Gretchen snorted. "How ridiculous," she said out loud. "I wouldn't stoop that low to go after a client." *Now, if he'd been a professional football player or maybe one of those delightful soccer boys, she might have touched a few muscles!*

Her glass was empty. Gretchen yawned. It had been a very long day. She grabbed the nearly full bottle and trudged toward her perfectly clean and fashionable bedroom. *I must suggest to Hal that they clean those police cars and maybe place a few pillows in the back seat.* She set the wine on the bedside table and removed her clothes. She headed toward the bathroom and grabbed her silk nightgown hanging on the door. She was even too fatigued to enjoy a relaxing bath.

As she began to remove her layers of makeup slowly, Gretchen studied her face. With the removal of each layer of store-bought beauty, her face lost all its color. She was pale. The dark circles under her eyes and the crow's feet at the side of her eyes were not complimentary. "Laugh lines, my butt. There's not one funny thing about these damn things."

She removed her lashes. "I'm an old woman. When did this happen?" *When I was being questioned by the detective? What is going on?*

Gretchen headed for her bed and took a very unlady-like swig from her bottle. She'd have to begin damage control tomorrow. She looked at her alarm clock. It was after midnight. She would do it today. She'd find out about her car parked at the church. She would assure her clients. She would call Marty. She had to save her business. *I only have my business. It's my life.*

Slowly, she crept into bed. Alone. *And when did this happen?* There had been men over the years, but lately

Gretchen Malloy was alone. Men would take a glancing touch now and then, in a crowded room, so they could use deniability as their cover. She'd smile appreciatively, but those men weren't in her bed at the end of the night. They weren't here to protect her.

"I don't need them," Gretchen whispered.

She took another rather large drink, returned the half empty bottle to the table and turned out the light. The room was dark. She yawned.

Her mind remained awake and filled with questions. *Today was ridiculous. Why did they pick on me? Why did they think I was after that boy? Maybe some woman had been with him? Or was someone after me? Was someone setting me up? Why did Trent's father remove that paper or whatever it was? Why did he lie and say I had been all over his son the night before? Did he say Trent didn't want to get married? I can understand that, but why didn't he want a big wedding? Everyone wants a wedding of their dreams, don't they? I wouldn't care, but as socially connected as this couple was it was mandatory. And why didn't Rhonda cry? I know what it feels like to lose someone you love. I cried, well only in private. No one needed to see me cry.*

Gretchen Malloy always thought everything was about her, that the sun did revolve around her little world. This time the heat was real. It just might be all about her. If she only knew why.

Chapter Four

There are no vampires roaming the streets in Kansas City, Missouri, at least the police department didn't recognize that the nocturnal creatures lived and killed unsuspecting grooms on their wedding day. There were stilettos that could make marks on the neck of said groom. The groom was dead either way from the vampire or the heels.

Mayor Hal Jacquard reached Gretchen's actual attorney on Sunday afternoon. John Palmer would come out of retirement to help a woman he'd known for so many years. He knew his son couldn't handle a murder trial if it came to that. They discussed the news coverage. Gretchen was featured on the front page of the city's newspaper. The story was on every television and radio news program as the city mourned a groom's death on his wedding day. When you added in murder, even the national news sources were highlighting the sensational Kansas City event. Hal and John were more concerned about how their friend would react to an older photo of herself. It was a rather bad shot of Gretchen at a gala a few years ago. Her hair was wind swept, and she had a demonic smile on her face. Obviously, she'd had way too many martinis that night and was resembling a character in a comic strip. The two professionals would recommend she stay in her apartment until the autopsy report was announced. They made sure her car was returned to her apartment parking space.

They trusted that their dear friend would never really commit murder; she'd talk about it, heck she might even plan it, but she'd never do it. Both men did agree she could bore you to death with her stories of exploits with men. They also agreed that most of the tales were probably real events from the past, a very active past. Gretchen Malloy was many things, but never a liar, or even an exaggerator. Her cup was full. She lived a life filled to the brim with experiences.

By Wednesday, Gretchen was stir crazy. She cleaned the kitchen twice. She dusted the entire apartment. There would be nothing for her housekeeper to do this week. While going through her closet, Gretchen melted into a puddle of tears. She ended up in a heap on the floor as she looked up through her clothing. No one, not one person had ever seen her cry like this, the ugly cry. Her reputation was in tatters, but she was grateful that Marty trusted her. She was still planning his event. She touched the hem of one of her dresses.

The lovely gold chiffon and satin gown had been worn years ago. She wasn't sure why she still had it hanging in an overly stuffed closet. She'd meant to donate it to one of the Junior League shops many times. *Stop fooling yourself, old girl. You know exactly why you still have it hanging in here.* The gown had been an integral part of a very special evening with one special man. *My, I haven't thought about him in years.* She was fooling herself again. She thought about him every day. Invariably, she would see a man with his build or those dazzling blue eyes, and she would think of him. He was the one who got away, well, she had been the one who walked away.

Gretchen swiped away the tears on her cheek. "No more crying," she announced. *There's no reason to feel sorry for yourself. You're Gretchen Malloy, and you're the best!* She touched the dress again. That night, they had danced for hours. He looked so handsome in his uniform. She chuckled. The actress Ginger Rogers used to say she danced every step her partner did, but in an evening gown and heels, and backwards. That was Gretchen's motto. She didn't need a man to give her value; she had her heels, very expensive ones!

She lifted herself slowly up from the floor. *Darn knees. No one is going to throw me into a pit of doom and desperation. I have work to do!* Over the years, Gretchen had planned campaign launches before, but this time she was planning everything for Marty. They'd been friends for years, way too many years to count. He had been her little sister's fiancé. There had been such joy in that relationship, and they always allowed Gretchen to share in the fun. *All those happy times died the day my little sister died on the way to her own wedding.*

Gretchen's sister had gone back to the house for one more thing before driving herself to the church. She remembered that day as if it was a couple of weeks ago instead of nearly three decades.

"Let me go get it, Amy," Gretchen had begged.

"No, silly. I know exactly where I left the blue garter. You'll never find it. Besides, you need to stay here and keep everybody under control. That's what you do best. I'll be back in a few minutes. We will get me in my dress, and I will march down that aisle." Amy had waved goodbye to Gretchen. She'd smiled from the car and blew her sister a kiss. Her long brown hair was blowing out from the open window. Her bright eyes sparkled with such joy. Her pink lips formed the last kiss she would ever receive from her. That's how she remembered her sister, young and beautiful, and filled with such love. Less than twenty minutes later, a driver coming down the wrong way on a one-way street, took Amy's life. He was drunk. Amy was dead.

Marty was devastated and inconsolable at the funeral. Amy did go down that aisle...in a casket. Gretchen held Marty, then her mother, and her father. She didn't have enough arms to hold all of them. There weren't enough tissues to wipe away the tears. She decided to never cry again, until last night's fiasco when one little tear escaped from her fortress. Today, she was openly weeping. She was not allowed to feel sorry for herself. As her own boss, it was forbidden.

She headed into the kitchen for a glass of wine when the phone rang. It was her retired attorney John Palmer.

"John? It's so nice of you to call."

"Hal and I talked, Gretchen. I'm going to be representing you, if it goes that far. I'll handle the police from now on."

Gretchen fell back on her bed in relief. "Oh, thank you, John. You have no idea how happy I am right now. I mean your son is fine, but he's not you."

The attorney laughed. "You put him through the ringer the other day. He needed that, but he doesn't need to get involved in this. The boy isn't ready. Besides, I know all the players."

"I thank you. Hal and you are two of my oldest friends in this city."

John Palmer cleared his throat. "Gretchen, I wanted you to hear this from me before the news breaks."

Gretchen looked up toward the ceiling. She knew she didn't kill Trent, but she still had her doubts that anyone else would realize that.

"Just spit it out, dear John. I can't stand any more drama," said the number one drama queen in the city.

"They finally released the autopsy results. All they told me was the boy was murdered by poison. Someone did take a heel and make those puncture wounds, but it was done postmortem. They won't be arresting you, but they may still name you as a suspect, just for looks. But I don't want you to worry."

"Really, John? Don't worry? I'm still a suspect. I'm not off the hook."

"But it is looking better."

Gretchen sighed heavily. "By whose perspective? The view out my window is stormy. What am I supposed to do while waiting for the good guys to apprehend the bad guy? How am I supposed to have a life, or continue my business with this cloud hanging over me?"

"It won't be much longer. The final reports will show that you couldn't have done it. The timing is all off. I also heard from one of the other investigators that someone saw a woman, with two champagne glasses, heading into the church with the groom. He was carrying a bottle. There's a witness that saw you fiddling with the flower girl's dress, something about a crooked bow. You were working."

"Hmm, well it seems like timing is the only reason I'm not in the clink right now. I also know the mayor." *Who was this woman with the champagne? Could she be the woman Trent's father had seen the night before?*

The lawyer didn't dare tell his client she was exactly right. Hal had stuck his neck out for Gretchen Malloy. Even though he only had one more year of his term, he was taking a chance. He must've had his reasons to use his clout with the police. One detective in particular didn't appreciate it. Hopefully, this report about a witness seeing some other woman would exonerate Gretchen completely.

"Gretchen, just stay below the radar for now."

Gretchen sniffed her disdain at that comment. "Do you know me, John? I walk into a room, and everyone notices me. I won't be a normal person."

"There is no fear of that happening," the attorney murmured. The woman could never be normal. No normal woman wore yoga gear with bangle bracelets and heels. Gretchen wore the ensemble to brunch. "Well, then, just take care. I'll check in with you tomorrow, or sooner, if I hear anything."

"I'll be waiting for your call." She hung up before he ended his goodbye. She grabbed the now opened wine bottle and turned it upside down. The liquid was just what she needed.

"They used a stiletto to make those marks," she said out loud. Stilettos were **her** signature style accessory. *How dare they use shoes against me! Who are you, and why are you trying to frame me?*

Gretchen took one more swallow of wine and brought the bottle with her into the bedroom. She began to search through her closet with one purpose in mind.

Where was that champagne and the two glasses? When she'd arrived to discover Trent sprawled on the floor, she saw no sign of another person, nor of the alcohol. But now she remembered smelling the lovely aroma of a really good bubbly. *Wait, there was something else in the air.* A woman's fragrance filled the usually stagnant church anteroom. *Maybe Trent was embraced by a well-wishing woman? The perfume would linger on his tux.*

"Where is my black hat? I'll need those black tights, the jacket, anything black. I'm going dumpster diving." On second thought, she'd grab any black clothing she was willing to discard. *Hmm, maybe the cheetah pants?* She smiled. *If one is going dumpster diving, one must dress well.*

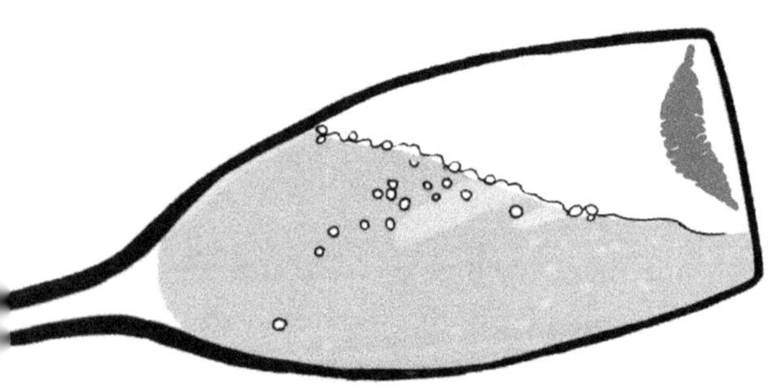

Chapter Five

Gretchen waited until midnight before arriving in the church's parking lot. Midnight is the perfect time to discover evidence in a murder. No one ever found any incriminating piece of evidence at one in the afternoon. Besides, no one would be around the church at the bewitching hour.

Gretchen's car neared the church. She turned off her headlamps. *What if the garbage truck had already removed the evidence? What if the woman who was trying to set me up has already fished out the glasses and maybe the bottle too?*

"It's still worth the chance I'm taking," she said in the darkness. "Come on old girl. You must do this."

She parked her car behind the back of the church and slowly made her way to the huge trash dumpster located closest to the murder location. Even with her heels on, the trash bin's height was a good foot above her. She needed something to stand on. In the dark, she blindly felt the pavement. *This is getting me absolutely nowhere.* In desperation, Gretchen finally turned on her flashlight. Nothing. There was absolutely nothing available to perch on.

Gretchen sauntered back to her car and drove it as close to the bin as possible. Standing on the hood of her vehicle, she carefully pushed up onto the side. She began her descent into the great unknown of the trash world and all things mushy and yucky. *I have never done anything this disgusting. Well, there was that weekend escape with the mud wrestler...*

"What was that?" Her heel met with a moving item. If she ran into an errant possum, she would faint. Then the animal would ravage her. Instead of prison, she would die of rabies. "Get it together, Gretchen. Look for those glasses and whatever else you can find to free yourself from prison."

Her gloved hand pulled away rubbish, including several brown bags from a fast-food restaurant. Her next treasure was the bride's bouquet. Gretchen looked it over carefully. Such a happy day became such a sad one. Something so beautiful was now so ugly. She remembered how Amy's bouquet had shriveled into a brown cluster of blooms. She had placed it on top of the churned dirt at the cemetery. Gretchen sighed and looked up at the stars. It was a clear night, filled with stars galore. One in particular seemed to be brighter than the others. "Amy, if that's you, I need your help right now. In fact, I just need you."

Gretchen purged through the occasional disposable coffee cups and catsup packets. The flashlight was soon covered with flying debris. She cleared it off. *Catsup.* Gretchen was hoping for a miracle and all she was finding was trash. "Human beings are animals. This is disgusting." The smell wasn't much better. She would need a long shower, followed by a longer bubble bath. A massage and sauna at the club would do the trick. "Will I ever be clean again?"

As she shuffled through the muck, she heard a small clink. It was the clink of her heel up against the glass. She lit her way and began to dig. As if she had discovered gold, the flashlight lit up a toasting glass as bright as a diamond. She fished around with her hand and picked up another flute just like the other. The second glass sported the distinctive mark on its rim of a woman's lipstick stain.

"Eureka! I've done it." Her eyes narrowed as she found a small clear item within the glass. *Hmm, what are you doing here?* Suddenly, the darkness was filled with light as though the sun was shining.

"What have you done, Ms. Malloy?" It was a familiar voice, one she preferred to never hear again. She would've hit her head up against the side of the container, but she couldn't take the chance of whatever slimy bug made his home in that side of the receptacle.

"I found the evidence you need, Detective Williams." She stretched her arms up in the air, showing him the glasses.

"Come out with your hands up and whatever you have."

Gretchen removed the smallest piece of evidence and stuck it down her shirt. "Oh, I hate this." The feel of the garbage seemed to be taking her in as though it was quicksand. *Now I'll need two showers.* She should have handed over her prize to the detective, but she didn't trust him yet. Internally, and very briefly, a debate pitched back and forth. *I should, but I can't. I have to keep this to myself until I can figure this all out.*

Two slender, gloved hands rose from the receptacle, holding two Waterford crystal champagne flutes. As four policemen and the detective came closer to her, Gretchen studied the glasses and committed every etched cut to memory. *I've seen this pattern recently, somewhere.* It would come to her, hopefully before she was sent up to the big house and became the girlfriend of a woman named Big Addie.

"You'll have to help me out," Gretchen called out.

The detective had on his own gloves by now as he grabbed the two glasses from her hands. He directed the other men to assist his suspect out of the trash.

By the time she was handcuffed, the detective had placed the glasses in an evidence bag and was examining the contents. He raised the bag in front of Gretchen's eyes.

"You want to tell me what these are?" His cool grey eyes only contained judgement once more.

Gretchen studied the two glasses from rim to stem and then from stem to rim. She took a second to compose her thoughts and suddenly remembered. "Hibernia."

Excuse me?"

Gretchen batted her lashes. "It's not a Lismore pattern. These glasses are too old. They are Waterford crystal for sure, so I'm thinking it may be the Hibernia pattern. We have an Irish crystal shop here in the area. We can call them. You know, sometimes, clients need an extra glass, or they come into the shop looking for other patterns that might--"

The detective shook his head dismissively. "Enough. Just stop talking. **We** aren't doing anything together, Ms. Malloy. You are coming back with us for more questioning."

"What about my car?" Gretchen pleaded. She hated the sound of her own voice. *I sound pathetic. I'm never pathetic, or weak, or afraid. But I am.*

"We will have it towed to the police lot."

"You will not. My baby will not be left overnight among criminal cars! I want to call my attorney right now. He lives down the street and will pick it up."

Williams handed the bagged glasses over to another detective.

"If not, I can call Mayor Jacquard again, Detective Williams. We both know how you love to see him. I just have this little feeling that he likes you too."

The detective's shoulders rose quickly as though he'd just heard a tower of glass crashing. As he turned to face her, his hands flew up in surrender. "Fine. Call your attorney to pick up your car, but you are still coming with us. Tell him that too."

Detective Williams returned to his car and watched the scene in front of him. Apparently, Gretchen Malloy could not speak without her hands. As a miniscule gesture of good faith, he instructed the officers to remove her cuffs. His number one suspect's hands flailed like waving kites, even the one that held the phone. He slowly lowered his head onto his steering wheel.

"Lord, why me? Why didn't Detective Ragland catch this one?" Gretchen Malloy was an irritant, a nag, and a talker. But she didn't seem to be a woman who would seek revenge. She seemed like a woman who was unrelenting and driven, not one who would dwell on being jilted. This entire case was about someone getting even with the groom. "Why does the woman talk so much?" His head struck the wheel two times. "And, she's innocent, isn't she?" He knew deep down in his gut that the woman couldn't murder a spider, but she was involved in some way. He just had to figure out how and why, and hopefully, the actual murderer would show his or her face. In the meantime, he'd proceed as he normally would, letting everyone think Ms. Malloy was the only suspect. His head remained resting on the wheel when he heard the tapping of nails on his car window. *Tink, tink, tink.* It was her.

Cuffed again, Gretchen wanted his attention. She was gaining his wrath. He lowered his window, his face showing displeasure, and perhaps rage. "What? What do you want?"

Gretchen's left eyebrow rose suggestively. "What I want is one thing, and what you will probably give me is entirely something else." She smiled sweetly.

"Ms. Malloy, you are trying my patience. What?"

"Will I be in your company for very long? I have a meeting in the morning. I need to make arrangements depending on how long you and I are together." Gretchen paused and smiled wider. "My, that sounded provocative, didn't it?" She added a wink for emphasis. *I was going to tell him where I've seen those champagne flutes, but he can be so disagreeable. He can figure it out on his own that the old pattern would've been in an older house, one that still held china and glassware from its previous owners.*

Williams moved his window up without answering. One of the other officers pushed her gently into a squad car. In the rearview mirror he watched her head carefully dodging the roof. His plans were to fingerprint her and get that all important mugshot. He chuckled. She'd be appalled when her fingers were dirtied and her photo wasn't perfect. Could he charge her with interference in a criminal investigation or maybe trespassing in a dumpster? Probably not, but she didn't know that. He needed for her to understand that he was in charge. She didn't need to know that he was only printing her and getting that mugshot for his own delight. He'd happily receive disciplinary action for the ruse. Maybe it would teach her a lesson. His thoughts turned to using the mugshot for target practice. His smile vanished. He heard her voice in his head, and his head throbbed in pain. He always performed his duties by the book, and yet she made him go rogue.

"That woman is driving me insane.

Chapter Six

Gretchen made her morning meeting, with no thanks to Detective Williams. She arrived back at her apartment at eight in the morning, with only a couple of hours to shower and scrub, and to repeat the showering and scrubbing, put herself together, and to grab a coffee, and small cheese quiche at her favorite Country Club Plaza coffee hangout. She had no time to pick it up, but the concierge at her building had the food and caffeinated drink waiting for her at his desk in the lobby. Her car was also waiting, thanks to John Palmer.

"What would I do without my men?" she asked herself as she drove to Marty's home. Martin Stanton and she maintained a wonderful friendship for several decades now. Her sister, Amy, Marty, and she were like three peas in a pod when they were younger. They were all inseparable in high school. Marty and Amy went off to college together on the East Coast, but Gretchen had selected one in California. By the time her sister and future brother-in-law graduated, Gretchen was working with a large event planner in Hollywood. Amy followed Marty as he went on to law school. Soon, the couple were planning their future life, and as soon as he graduated, their wedding. That day changed everything for all of them.

When Marty called her three months ago detailing his plans to run for a United States Senate seat, Gretchen was supportive yet surprised. Marty wanted her to plan his launch party and to be there with him when he announced such a great undertaking. He had always been such a shy man, but he had changed in the last few years. He had finally met someone who was significantly transforming him with happiness. Her name was Olivia.

Marty met Olivia in New York City. She was on the board of a charity, and Marty was attending one of their functions. He said she was witty, beautiful, and she was just what he needed after all of these years of loneliness. They were married within the year. She was a forty-something widow with two grown sons and her own trust fund and foundation.

Marty had explained, "She doesn't need my money. She has her own. She just wants to be with me. It is a miracle."

When her almost brother-in-law's voice quivered with emotion, Gretchen had shed one little tear, not enough to say she was crying. "I'm so happy for you, Marty. You've waited all your life for this kind of happiness again. Embrace it."

"You'll love her, Gretchen. She is the most amazing woman I have ever met. I hope you two will become friends." Gretchen promised she would try, and try she would even if it killed her. *Marty needs to be happy, and I'll do everything to make sure he is.*

As Gretchen drove by the mansions in the Kansas City area, she recalled that first meeting. Olivia had been everything that Marty had described, and yet there was just something about her. Gretchen had written off her feelings because of her concern for Marty's heart, but those feelings kept nagging her thoughts. The woman wasn't easy to be with; she was not one you'd want for a girlfriend.

After all of these years of enjoying the occasional luncheon date with a woman friend, Gretchen finally acquired a real girlfriend in the form of Lily Schmidt Pierce and her assistant Abby. Those two women touched her heart when others couldn't, or wouldn't. Abby had the energy of more than four people, and she envied Lily's organizational skills. Although Gretchen had determined Lily had an obsession with post-it notes. She saw Abby now and then, but she missed Lily. She missed their nights out at a theatre or their evenings in with a bottle of wine and a pizza. She missed Lily's curly hair and curvy body. The woman wasn't perfect, especially when she laughed too hard and snorted. And those two girls never treated her badly, even when she was pretentious with them. They were always professional, and at least to her face, they were pleasant.

If anything, Gretchen didn't appreciate that Lily had moved away after marrying the delicious Devlin Pierce. The little florist had also reintroduced her to carbs, and now Gretchen had to work out like a fiend to keep her legs lean and her hips from becoming their own amusement attraction.

On the other hand, Olivia Stanton was svelte. While here in Kansas City for the first time, she played tennis daily at the club. She was gaining attention; most members were gossiping about her looks. She was flawless with long brown hair, a size zero figure, and legs that went on forever... even without heels! She was a bright, articulate heiress who could discuss any subject without offending anyone. She was the perfect country club member and would make the perfect senator's wife.

Once at Marty's, Gretchen spoke with security, and the gates opened on the long driveway. *But she has that wimpy handshake.* Gretchen disliked any woman who couldn't shake a hand. *Certainly, she didn't expect me to kiss her hand, did she?*

The event planner picked up her briefcase and exited her car. Today's meeting would be a walk-through in preparation for the caterer and with Marty's growing political staff.

Gretchen put aside the events surrounding her as Marty greeted her with open arms and an open door. "Honey, how are you? Are you living through all that chaos from the wedding?"

His arms enveloping her brought her confidence back. She kissed him lightly on the cheek, careful to not leave any lipstick on his face. "You know me. I live through everything, and I'm better for it."

"That's my girl. Come on in. I want you to meet my campaign manager and the head of my security team. Olivia has brunch by the pool for all of us."

Gretchen never tired of this home. Marty's mom and dad always hosted all of the high school events here. It was like her second home. The ivy-covered brick mansion had one of the most amazing flying staircases with a large portrait of Marty's mother at the top of the first floor landing. A Tiffany chandelier hung from the second story down into the foyer. A few changes had been made over the years, and thankfully Marty had removed his mother's old brocade sofa in the formal reception room to the right of the massive front door. She glanced at the china cabinet filled with the best of the best, including Irish crystal. *I'd bet my entire collection of gold bracelets that two glasses are missing. Well, not the bracelet Antonio bought me in Rome, but certainly the rest.* Gretchen visually and mentally took inventory of what was new in the room. She noticed that Olivia had added several photos. On top of Marty's mother's grand piano were photos of Olivia and Marty in Hawaii, another in Times Square, a wedding photo, and another of the couple kissing in front of the Eiffel Tower. There were a few candid photos of young men who were possibly Olivia's sons. Marty walked ahead as Gretchen stopped to look at one in particular. She knew Olivia had two sons. Three young men were celebrating their graduation, two looked virtually alike, the other was Trent Hampton.

"Gretch, are you coming?"

Marty's call brought her out of shocked haze. "Holy, Moly," she whispered out loud. Lily used that phrase frequently, and it was creeping into her vocabulary every now and then. It was definitely something to say when you had no other words to use.

Gretchen nonchalantly balanced her phone at her waist for a quick photo of the three boys and walked quickly behind Marty toward the pool area.

An attractive younger man greeted her with his hand extended and a wide smile on his lips. "I'm Ryan Marley, Martin's campaign manager."

Gretchen's professional face was sweet and smiling. She surveyed his haircut and wardrobe, each very expensive. His hands were soft and well-manicured. There was a hint of an accent, perhaps the blending of a couple areas of the country. He had his own look. She noticed he began his tour of her body and face with a look into her eyes. As he stood back, she knew he was looking over her clothes and especially her jewelry. Once he finished his appraisal, he pointed at her shoes. She had decided to wear these specific red shoes with an animal print today because Marty seemed to love them.

"Do you always wear heels?"

"If I leave the apartment, they are on my feet. They are my look," Gretchen answered.

"Ah, I heard that. Well, you are a wonder woman, just like Marty said," Ryan complimented. "We have a limited staff right now, but we will be growing after the announcement. We have a few others handling our social media." The young manager pointed over to a table on the other side of the pool where three young staffers worked on their laptops. In her mind, all three were dressed too casually to be working on a national government race, and they looked like babies. *I really am getting old. I could be their mother...their grandmother.* Gretchen shivered with the realization.

Olivia greeted her with air kisses on each cheek and poured her a much-needed mimosa. Her entire evening spent in Detective Williams' company had been painstaking. Usually when she spent that kind of time with a man she might be tired in the morning, but she certainly wasn't unhappy. This morning she was exhausted and hiding the remaining black dye on her fingers. She made a mental note to speak to her attorney about how she had been treated. There had been quite a bit of laughing as though she had been the target of a terrible prank. But she had more to worry about than a bad photo and blackened fingers.

Olivia led her over to a lovely buffet of breakfast items and an assortment of seafood.

"The scallops were flown in this morning Gretchen, so they are as fresh as you can get them in middle America," Olivia remarked as she served her own plate. "Please, eat. I'm sure you're starving."

Actually, I can use a good meal, but why would I naturally be starving? Is the tiny woman making some crack about my curves? Stop it, Gretchen. Why am I feeling insecure? The late nights at the police department are cracking my resolve.

Gretchen did her own homework. She researched Olivia when Marty first announced he had fallen in love. She also researched the very ambitious Ryan Marley when she was first given his name. He came from a good family, one who had attended Ivy League schools for generations. Surprisingly, Ryan had been recommended for the position by Olivia. She had raved about his skills until Marty relented and hired him. Ryan had his eyes on the future candidate, except when he was looking at Olivia. *I don't like how they're exchanging knowing looks. They're either keeping secrets or protecting the future of a possible senator.*

Gretchen was placing a lovely piece of pineapple on her plate when Marty announced the arrival of his head of security. She knew the man was a former secret service agent. Apparently, he had been in the military as well.

"Here he is. You need to get some breakfast. Gretchen, as soon as you get your food, come meet my head of security, Charles Alexander."

China clinked against a serving dish. Gretchen dropped her plate onto the table in front of her. Her mouth was suddenly dry, and she was no longer hungry. She slowly turned around to see the man, a man who was equally shocked to see her.

"I think you're going to enjoy this, Chance. This is our planner, and one of my best friends, Gretchen Malloy. I've known her since high school, and I believe you two went to college together, right?" Marty clapped his hands, totally entertained by the dazed looks on his two friends' faces.

Time did stand still, transporting Gretchen into a scene in an old black and white movie. She was Rosalind Russell or Grace Kelly; he was Cary Grant, always Cary Grant. She tried to smile. She felt her one lip curl up. Apparently, it was looking more like a snarl as the man returned a questioning look. But then he smiled. He smiled that smile he always had only for her. If she had been a southern belle, she would've swooned.

He came to her and stood inches away. His scent was fresh soap. She could feel the warmth of his breath and his body heat now surrounding her. She had suddenly become a revolving moon, and he was her sun. He was always her sun, filling her with a passionate heat and fire that seemingly never could be extinguished.

"Gretchen." He turned back to Marty. "Have you enjoyed your little surprise, Marty?" Chance's tone and lack of thanks caused the senatorial hopeful to back away quickly from the two former college sweethearts.

Charles "Chance" Alexander returned his attention to his first love. His eyes searched her face, watched her lips.

"How are you? It's been so long." His gaze went down the length of her body, landing on her footwear. "Wow, you're still wearing those killers?"

Gretchen flinched at his question and terminology. She nodded. As soon as she could finally shake off the shock of Marty's little reunion, she forced her mouth into a smiling shape. "I'm fine. Shocked but fine. You look good." He looked amazing, but she wouldn't admit that. There was no way he could keep that body looking like that without some sort of injection or the involvement of a voodoo priestess and her concoction of a youth potion.

He wrapped both arms around her and whispered into her ear. "Those heels might be dangerous, but they sure do make your legs look as good as ever. I used to love those legs wrapped around me. I can't believe we will be working together."

"Yes, working together," Gretchen murmured. He smelled so good. He felt so good. He had to bring back those memories. *I have to get it together. It's been years. The past won't become the future. It just won't. It can't.* He didn't deserve one more second of thought while she did her job. "We do need to get started on this meeting. Grab yourself something to eat. "She pulled away, nonchalantly grabbed her plate, and finished filling it. She headed to the table without looking back at him. She hid her shaking hands and used the tabletop to bolster her arm as she ate. Memories of his touch controlled the rest of her body and began to take her on a trip down memory lane with all the feelings of that one great lost love. Yes, she used to wrap her legs... She needed to maintain a facade of control, a modicum of strength. *Decorum, Gretchen. You are working.*

She was Gretchen Malloy, and years ago she hadn't been so mature. It used to be so difficult to keep him at bay. But she needed to do her job despite Chance's beautiful eyes. Of course, then there were those lips and that hair to disregard. He also had those broad shoulders, strong arms, and those long fingers. She had to stick to her job.

"As soon as Chance gets over here, we will begin," Gretchen announced. "We have quite a bit of work to do. I have some ideas about the decorations around the pool. I will also need the final guest list. Have the invitations gone out?" She directed her attention to young Ryan. He shuffled through his papers. Olivia pointed to assorted notes to his right.

Through bites of food, the meeting progressed with the campaign manager and the event planner taking on the lion's share of the work. Gretchen became Ms. Professional, and her persona took control. She smiled occasionally, but never directly at Chance, her former love. He was the love of her life; he was the man who got away. *Why is all this happening to me at the same time?*

"Where is the best location for you to make the announcement? I was thinking here by the pool, but if it is warm, I would suggest some cool air units or misters around the perimeter. We could have flowers floating, elegant, not cheesy."

"Excuse me, but we need to think of the security difficulties with that location." Chance finally inserted himself into the discussion.

Gretchen looked over her glasses. "Is there some sort of threat to Marty?"

"Let's say I have some concerns," Chance answered. His low rumbling voice of a former Marine shook Gretchen to her toes. "We have had a few threats, and the other day we had a suspicious package."

"Oh, posh," Olivia said with a laugh. "I told you it might have been something I ordered. I lose track of my purchases. Besides, who would want to hurt Martin?"

Gretchen watched Olivia's mouth as she said her husband's name. No one that really knew Marty called him Martin. Except for Olivia.

"Exactly," Marty added. "No one. I think you are overly concerned, Chance."

"I don't think I am." Chance looked over the table to Gretchen. His eyes showed his concern, and his voice dripped with annoyance. "You hired me to keep you safe. Let me do my job." His tone dripped with a hint of danger, sending cold shivers down Gretchen's back despite the lovely warm day.

"We can move it inside, in fact that would work better," Gretchen suggested. Chance had some obvious concerns, and she would follow his lead, just this one time. Heaven knew she never had done it years ago, but this time would be different, especially if Marty's life was at stake. "We can clear the living room, keep the piano, place a podium in front of the west wall of windows. The cocktail party can be around the pool with a sound system for the overflow guests. Would that work, Chance?"

"Yes, perfect. The awning over the windows will shield any view from the fence lines. We could work up a plan on that together."

Gretchen placed her eyeglasses next to her laptop. She liked the sound of working together. *Is my heart beating faster? Are my eyelashes fluttering uncontrollably? Maybe I ate too much bacon? Old girl, get yourself together.* "Olivia, Marty, is there anything else we need to discuss?"

Marty shrugged off her question. Olivia pushed her chair back from the table. "I would like your advice on what I should wear, Gretchen. I have a few dresses hanging in the study for you to review. If you would follow me."

Ryan chuckled. "I suppose we have just ended this meeting." He threw a file folder on the table. Olivia shielded a contemptuous snarl, but Gretchen and Chance noticed her action. *Ah, Olivia doesn't like him? Perhaps the lady is acting? Why did she need to?*

Gretchen smiled and began to trail behind Olivia as she strolled into the house. She followed her into the study that housed all of Marty's trophies from high school and college. His degrees were displayed along the walls.

"This place reminds me of a museum. This room in particular is too dark for my taste. But if he wins, we'll move to Washington, and perhaps I can make him sell this albatross. He needs to purge himself of the past. Here are the gowns." Olivia pointed to four dresses hanging along a drapery rod. The designer items ranged from short cocktail dresses to lavish gowns. "What do you think, Gretchen?"

Gretchen's mouth was still involuntarily wide open in shock at this home being addressed as an albatross. *Ah, so it would be easy for you to throw all this away? You want him to forget his past, but he hired me? Just because something is filled with memories didn't give someone the right to come in and destroy the past at the snap of her fingers. I know what I don't like about her now. Maybe I should punch her out? No, violence even warranted never solved anything.* Gretchen took a few deep breaths and smiled. She looked over each dress carefully. *Perhaps, Olivia is feeling a little lost without any attention directed at her? Meeting old friends can be icy for a spouse feeling less than a warm welcome. I'll try to do better.*

"You have such amazing taste. Any of these lovelies would work, but I would probably go with either a black cocktail or a deep jewel color with your skin tone. This designer's collection is impeccable." Gretchen held out the skirt of a deep navy gown that featured a jeweled belt.

"I do have beautiful skin." Olivia seemed distracted as she ran her hand down her neck. She threw her long hair back in an exaggerated fashion. "Of course, you are right. I would look good in anything."

"Yes." Gretchen wanted to say so much more, but one word sufficed. She watched as Marty's wife fingered each dress and touched the fabric as though they were lotion upon her hand.

Am I anything like your sister?"

Gretchen blinked twice. She pursed her lips and bit down hard. *What did she just say?* "Excuse me?" Gretchen stalled to formulate an answer.

"I asked if I'm anything like your sister, the dead one?"

Gretchen's heart fluttered, its quick beating blended with her irregular breathing. *How dare she?* "I only have, well had one, and yes, she is dead."

"I'm asking if I'm like Amy because Martin speaks of

her often. I never could understand why or how he could possibly wait decades to marry for the first time. At first, I thought he must be gay, but then as I came to know him, I realized he was just a very sweet man. He was so lonely for so long. Am I like her?" Olivia's rambling speech concluded. Gretchen was mesmerized by the woman's lips in some surreal scene of admission.

No, you are nothing like Amy. Amy was always mannerly and so kind. She made me look like Satan's daughter. Amy was joy and happiness mixed in a package decorated with bows. Gretchen clutched her left hand until her nails dug into her skin. She must treat Olivia as though she was a client. "Olivia, I believe Marty fell in love with you. It's been so many years. I don't believe he compared you to anyone."

"Ah, well that's a relief. Thank you for your input. I suppose that's it for today so we will see you next week for the final menu meeting, unless you are in jail again." Olivia laughed at her own joke as she threw back her long main of hair. "Thank you for all you are doing for Martin's night. He will be an amazing senator."

Gretchen chose to say absolutely nothing. She needed to leave, now. She followed after Olivia as though she were a lap dog. The three men were still seated discussing some numbers from some poll when Gretchen collected her computer and notes into her briefcase, placing it and her purse on the chair. "Have a good day, and I will see you all next week. Marty, call me if you need anything."

He came to her side quickly and pecked the side of her cheek. "And you call me if you need anything. This will all blow over. No one really thinks you killed that boy."

Gretchen noticed Olivia had not returned to the poolside, so it was her opportunity for a certain question. "Did Olivia's sons know Trent Hampton?"

"Yes, they were friends much like Amy, you, and me. In fact, Trent was just here the other day, before the wedding visiting Olivia. They were extremely close. She's taking it hard even though she doesn't show it, and she's concerned about your involvement."

"Oh, I'm sure she is," Gretchen admitted even though her answer was vague. *Let Marty figure out if Olivia is upset about Trent's death or my troubles?* It was too soon to ask how close they all really were, including the mother of Trent's friends. "You know me, Marty, I always end up on my feet. I'll be in touch."

Chance came around the table and to her side. "I'll walk you out, besides, I need to check the camera at the front gate."

Chance Alexander hadn't changed one bit over the years, Gretchen realized. He didn't wait long before he asked her what she knew was coming. He had just shut the front door behind him. "What's in your little head? I know you have something cooking up there, and it isn't some recipe you are making for dinner."

Gretchen walked a little faster, her heels making noise on the brick driveway. "I cook."

"You do not."

She reached her car door and opened it, choosing not to face him, not to look at that beautiful, chiseled chin, those eyes, that thin sculpted nose. *Stop it, woman.* "Sometimes,

I make soup, and I made crescent rolls a few times. That's baking.

"You popped open the container and threw them in the oven. So what is up? What did you see?"

Finally, Gretchen turned to face the beautiful man. His hair was now completely silver, hers wasn't. "My dead groom was a childhood friend of Olivia's sons."

"Apparently."

"My dead groom was having a secret fling with someone."

Chance grimaced. "You know that for sure?"

"Yes." Gretchen threw her bags into the car and began to slide in.

"And how are you sure? Did the police tell you that or are you just speculating?"

She shut the car door quickly, leaving Chance standing alone, his hands thrown up. She shielded her eyes with her dark sunglasses. He was yelling something about some hardheaded behavior. She slowly let the window down. Lowering her shades, she said, "I know for certain, because I always know when someone is cheating. I know for sure because I am Gretchen Malloy. I know everything in this city."

The event planner placed her car in gear and began to drive slowly around the man now shaking his head. She looked back once to see him still standing in place. Something was going on, and if the head of security wasn't going to help her then he needed to just get out of the way. Just like he did years ago.

Chapter Seven

By eleven the next morning, Gretchen had a massage and a few minutes in the sauna. After claiming she had a hair emergency, she weaseled into her favorite salon for a wash and blow out. While her hair was professionally styled and dried, Gretchen had so many thoughts. She desperately needed a plan. In her first of many formulated ideas, she texted the photographer and videographer from the wedding. Of course, the police had confiscated film and photos, but Gretchen knew that any professional worth their salt had backups either on their computer or in the cloud. All she needed was one clue, one speck of evidence hidden that only she could spot. After all, she was the queen of details.

After arriving home, Gretchen looked inside her refrigerator and laughed. "Old girl, Chance is right. You have never cooked, and you've never properly stocked a refrigerator." She closed the door and reached for her car keys and purse. It was time to head out for some real food.

As she opened her door, she was stopped by the wall of police. Dressed in a white fitted shirt with his collar void of any restricting tie, stood Detective Williams. His arm straightened, extending her a piece of paper that looked very official. "We have a warrant to search your apartment, Ms. Malloy. You need to stand in the hallway."

Gretchen grabbed the document. She threw back her

now perfect hair and lifted her chin in confidence. *So you want to play hardball, detective? You've never played with me.* She smiled at her own play on words. "Better than that, I'll leave. I'm going out for lunch. Call me if you need anything." She flipped her hand back in a goodbye wave as she pushed through the grouping of police.

As she approached the elevator, the door opened to reveal another man. Chance Alexander impeded her progress. "I'm going out for lunch, and don't try to stop me."

He waved her in and pressed the button to take them down. "How about I take you to lunch? I imagine the police will be awhile, unless you have become very organized."

She folded her arms over her chest. "My closet is immaculate."

"Ah, well then, they won't be there all day. We can take my car. I have it parked out front."

She said nothing. She still hadn't accepted his offer. Of course, she would, but she didn't want him to think she was easy. She smiled at that thought. *Well, Chance knew me when I wasn't.* "And, where exactly are you taking me, Agent Alexander?"

Chance opened the door for her. "It is a secret, and I haven't been an agent for two years now. I'm retired from that world."

Gretchen smirked. "And yet you knew that the police were going to search my place today. You always thought of yourself as the white knight sweeping in to protect little old me. I don't need you."

Chance closed the car door hard. Instead of expletives shouted, Gretchen was surprised to hear his laughter as he walked to the driver's side and entered the car. "I know you don't need me. Marty has major league contacts now so he's the one who suggested this rescue, which you obviously don't really need." Chance leaned his head over so he could gaze into her eyes. "But, a knight always protects his queen."

When he placed his sunglasses on his face, Gretchen's heart flip-flopped. *His queen indeed!* Not only did Chance ooze gallantry, he was the most attractive older man she had ever seen. *James Bond has nothing on him.* As he drove, she noticed his tanned forearms, the lack of rings, and his medical emergency bracelet.

"You still can't eat nuts."

He smiled as he turned onto one of the Country Club Plaza's streets. "And you have a great memory."

"It hasn't been that long." Gretchen knew she was lying, but she hoped he would think she was pretending that time does fly by quickly.

"But it has. Decades." The last word lingered on the air like a brick falling from a six-story building. Splat.

"So, two years retired? What have you been doing with yourself?"

Chance concentrated on his driving. It had been several years since he had been in Kansas City, Missouri on a security detail with the first President Bush. "I finally bought that sailboat, and I just stayed on the water for over a year. I visited every island in the Caribbean, even Cuba. After that trip, I sailed down to the beaches of South

America and then back again. When Marty asked me to come work for him, I was ready."

"Well, you ended up with a killer tan. You look rested."

Chance smiled. "Thank you, and you look amazing. After all of these years G, you still have it."

Her heart was ready to fly out of her chest and pass a jetliner in the sky. He had called her G, his very own nickname for her. No one else had given her a nickname, and no one else dared. *Wait, didn't Lily and her husband call me a stiletto terrorist? But that's not a nickname. It's an endearment!*

Gretchen diverted the conversation away from herself, away from the endearments that could pull her toward him. "How did you meet Marty?"

Chase continued to drive through the traffic confidently. "He was a friend of one of my Marine brothers. He liked to play golf. I liked to play golf. You know how that goes."

Gretchen nodded and rolled her eyes. *I know, and I remember. An opportunity to play a round of golf would always trump an afternoon with me.* Chase slowed the vehicle. Gretchen looked out to see the parking garage they were entering.

"You are taking me to the Nelson Art Gallery?"

"I remember you saying it was one of your very favorite places to go on a day off."

Gretchen sighed. "I said that years ago."

He pulled the car in and parked. "They have a lovely place for lunch."

"Yes, I often bring clients here."

"Good, let's go. I'm starving."

Gretchen didn't wait for him to come around to her side. "Some things never change. You were always starving," she muttered. He ran to her door.

"You should let me get that for you."

"You were always a gentleman, but I'm not a weak little female." Yet, inside she was giggling like a schoolgirl who was escorted by the captain of the football team. *Keep it together, woman. Stay strong.*

Chance offered her a hand and lifted her up. "And I never said you were. We both know who we are, but let me give you a few hours of nothingness, a few hours of forgetting everything around us."

Gretchen smiled. *Wouldn't that be nice if life could be that simple?* In the last few days, she had been educated once again that the world could spiral out of rotation and throw you on your backside in less than a minute. She would try to forget just this once.

Once inside, they were seated in the courtyard. Gretchen always marveled at the beauty of this place. Its tall tan columns and arches surrounded the diners. Trees in clay pots were placed strategically affording some privacy. It was a courtyard as beautiful as any in Venice, Florence, or Rome, all here in Kansas City. In the middle of the tiled floor stood a grand simple fountain, the spraying water soothing as it echoed in the great room. Up above was the mother of all skylights emitting sunlight into a beautiful sham of alfresco dining. Its elegance and romance spoke to

Gretchen's heart. *Chance still knows me, and he can still hurt me. Don't forget that!*

"You know when I have a client who is particularly tense, I bring them here to give them a little down time. Is that what you are really doing?"

"Taking your mind off of everything? Is it working?" With his smile, her heart melted.

Gretchen giggled as though she was twenty-one again, sitting across from a gorgeous boy who treated her as though she was Miss America. "A little. Thank you. So Marty knew about the search warrant?"

Chance nodded his head. Gretchen Florence Malloy hadn't changed after all. She just couldn't turn off that little brain of hers. She never could. "Marty thought you might need moral support when the judge who signed off on it called him to give him a head's up."

Gretchen leaned in. "A head's up? I don't understand."

"The judge knew you were planning the campaign launch at the house. He was concerned that it might color people's opinion of Marty. You know Marty. Once you are his friend he doesn't waiver. He believes in you, and so do I."

Chance looked quickly down at his menu. He didn't see her smile or hear her whisper a thank you. She didn't realize how much she needed to hear those words that those two special men believed in her innocence. It was laughable that she was innocent when it came to the ways of the world, but she was not a murderer.

Gretchen glanced down at the lunch selections. The words were blurry. She couldn't read one word. *I can't even see the words*. Reaching into her purse, she grabbed her glasses and saw the plastic bag hidden within. She could feel Chance watching her every move. It was perhaps an old holdover from his secret service days. Suddenly, she was warm, and it wasn't a hot flash. Those days were long gone. This was a much different kind of heat, one that was familiar. *Steady, girl. You can get burnt again.*

As a distraction to her growing passion, Gretchen searched for something bright and blingy. She couldn't see any of the jewelry of the women at the table just a few feet away from them, but as Chance lifted his menu and set it on the table, his medical bracelet caught her eye and engaged her brain. *Trent hadn't been wearing his bracelet. Of course, he wouldn't wear it on his wedding day if he wanted to appear perfect. Besides, if he had an allergy or ailment, his parents and his bride would've known and alerted that there was a medical problem. Had he left it at home? Wait.*

Gretchen casually opened her purse again and glanced at the piece of evidence hidden in her purse. *Yes! There's a small link from his bracelet. He did have it on. But why would someone tear it off of him?* She tapped her foot on the tile. *They wanted to buy them some time with the police, and to blame her. They were framing her. But who?*

Even though her foot was tapping nervously under the table, Gretchen portrayed a woman in control. Casually placing her glasses on her nose, Gretchen could read her choices. "Marty has to be the sweetest man on the face of the earth. Olivia is a lucky woman."

"Sometimes, and at other times I think she is a shrew," Chance admitted freely. "Marty doesn't see that side of her. I'm thinking I'll have the sirloin salad."

"I'm looking at the quiche and a salad. You know, Marty never did see the bad or ugly in anyone. I've always thought that's his one bad trait. It's a flaw really."

"You may be right." The server joined them, taking their orders. For the next hour, the conversation was filled with reminiscing and mundane information.

They were enjoying desserts of fresh berries and sorbet when Gretchen broached the subject that had been on the edge of her tongue throughout lunch. "You never married?"

Chance looked up and smiled sweetly. "That took you a few minutes before you asked."

Gretchen Malloy never blushed, but she was warm again. She wanted to blurt out that he should answer her question, but she just stared at him and tried not to think about those gorgeous eyes. "Well?"

"I did, and we are divorced. We were together almost ten years, and before you ask, I have a daughter." Chance stopped briefly. "She lives in Virginia Beach, and I'm actually going to be a grandfather sometime next month."

Gretchen clutched at her necklace in shock. "You? A grandfather?"

"Yep," he answered proudly. "I really can't wait. I've waited so long to spoil some little kid. I want to do it all, you know, change the diapers, rock the baby, teach him how to throw a baseball."

Without thinking, Gretchen reached for Chance's hand and held it. "You do know you have to wait on the baseball, right?"

"I know. I just can't wait."

"Chance, what if he is a she?"

"Then she is going to be the first woman in the major leagues," he answered confidently. "Or she can do whatever she wants to do. I don't care, as long as the baby is healthy."

"Your daughter, is she there by herself?"

Chance looked at Gretchen's hand. She pulled it back slowly. "She's happily married to a Navy guy."

Gretchen's eyebrows rose in surprise. "You allowed your daughter to marry into the Navy? Marine, what happened to you?"

"I became soft, and she loves him. He is a nice guy for a sailor."

"Ah, your little girl talked you into it. Women have always been your weakness, Charles Alexander."

Chance's smile faded. "As I remember it, there was only one woman who made me weak in the knees."

In his face, Gretchen could still see that disappointment from decades ago. She remembered that night as if it was yesterday. He had asked her to be his wife, to go with him to his first assignment in the Marines. *He promised me the world, but I never wanted to join the Marines.* She had smiled, laughed, and said no to him. She turned her head away when she saw him cry. *What a fool I was.*

"I'm sorry," she whispered. "I've always been sorry that I hurt you."

His voice was as low as hers as the server brought the bill. "I'm sorry I hurt you too."

After a few minutes of awkward silence, Gretchen's demeanor changed, her persona of Gretchen Malloy appeared. "Thank you so much for this lovely lunch. You have been such a dear to do this."

Chance heard the change in tone, watched the actress performing. "I guess we should get going. I need to go back to work, and you need to see what shape your apartment is in." He was up and around to her chair before she could protest. She looked up to thank him, but something, rather someone caught her eye.

"That's a couple of my very dear former clients, Nonni Weston and Bea Collier over there. I must say hello or they would be offended. Contacts are everything in my world."

Chance nodded. He understood completely what kind of world Gretchen lived in. He waited for her by the table as she waved to the two women and sauntered toward them. He watched as the smiling women, the unresponsive women, recognized Gretchen, and in that recognition, they turned their chairs and their backs on her. Gretchen stopped in mid-stride and turned. Her head was down when she returned to Chance's side.

"Let's go, please." She grabbed his hand and quickly paraded out, silently pulling him behind her.

Chance knew better, even after all of these years, than to say anything. Her heels made an obnoxious clicking sound on the marble, and echoed even louder in the parking garage. She still held his hand tightly. Occasionally, she wiped away a strand of blowing hair. Or was it a tear?

He opened the car door. She muttered a thank you. Once Chance was inside, he placed his right hand on her left shoulder. "G, it will be fine. You don't need people like that."

Her face turned quickly to face him. "Oh, but you are so wrong. You've never understood that fact. I do need people like that to survive. My business won't survive without people exactly like that. Without them, I'm a broken clown. Please take me home."

Chance realized that Gretchen was still Gretchen. She hadn't changed over all of these years, but he had. He wouldn't mourn her this time. He would leave Kansas City in a few weeks to welcome a grandchild into his life, and that would be enough. It would be enough, wouldn't it?

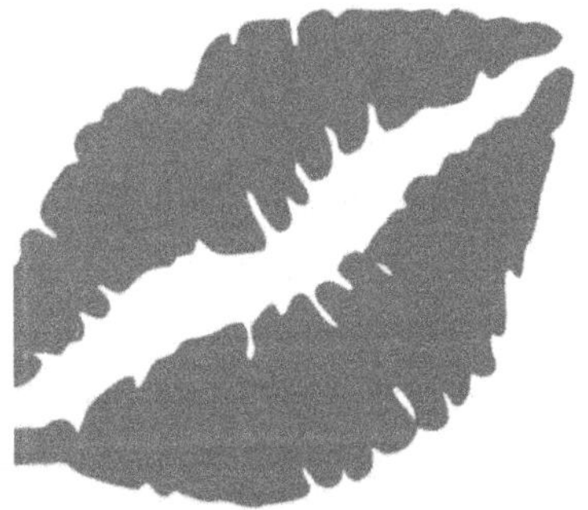

Chapter Eight

Gretchen entered her apartment and immediately called Natalie, her housekeeper. Natalie was on speed dial, and within an hour was putting the home back together again. The police left chaos in their wake, searching for something.

She noticed her bedroom had taken the brunt of the invasion. Her closet had been ransacked. Her makeup had been assaulted. Each lipstick had been displaced, and Gretchen knew exactly why. She usually had them organized alphabetically, and by color.

Why didn't they just ask me?

"Natalie, I'm going out on the balcony to do a little work." Gretchen and her laptop had a lot of work to do. First, she pulled up a designer's site to make sure she was right, and of course she was. The shade of lipstick on the flutes was 406, Millicent Rose. At over forty dollars, it was one of the more expensive lip colors in a lovely shade of pink. She had noticed Olivia wearing the same color at the meeting.

"Olivia, what other secrets are you keeping?"

The photographer and videographer had sent her links to the few photos and videos that had been taken prior to the murder. She needed help to look over all the details. Picking up her phone, Gretchen called one of her favorite florists.

"Abby, bestie number two, I need you." After a little conversation and a lot of compromise, Abby agreed to stop by Gretchen's apartment on her way home.

A couple of hours later, Natalie had the apartment back in shape and left the apartment as Abby walked through the living room and onto the balcony.

"What is the big deal?" she asked as she plopped down in the chair next to Gretchen. The coordinator's eyes were glued intently on her computer screen. Finally, she looked up after Abby sighed twice.

"Someone is framing me for murder. That's the big deal!" Gretchen placed her glasses down on the patio table. "I need help to look over these photos and this video from the wedding the other day. I've only gotten as far as the footage before the arrival of the wedding party at the church."

Abby grabbed the computer. "You mean the wedding where you found the dead groom?"

Gretchen sat back in her chair for the first time in hours. Her lower back was killing her. *Aging is not for the weak.*

"You know, I do miss Lily."

Abby looked up over the laptop. "I do too. Do you want my help or not?"

"I do, and you aren't as nice as Lily."

Lily owned Lily's Flower Shop, and Abby was its manager. Recently, Lily married and moved to Virginia, far away from flower deliveries and brides with unrealistic budgets and grand dreams. Lily was also Gretchen's very best friend, and her partner in the Pierce and Malloy

Detective Agency. The agency wasn't licensed, nor was it based in reality, but together they had surveilled a drug dealer and taken down a terrorist. Abby was a good fill-in for her absent friend, and the two florists were the only people she had run into in a long time who were unaffected by Gretchen's social standing in the city or her pull with clients.

Abby watched Gretchen. She looked tired. Her usual large statement pieces of jewelry were missing. With her eyes closed, Abby could see a vulnerability. This murder had shaken the usually confident woman and left her looking more like a normal human being. Seldom was the woman silent, but the more Abby was around her, she discovered that Gretchen Malloy wasn't just irritating, aloof, and irrational. The famed extraordinary planner had a heart, and the size of it was far greater than anyone knew. So she ignored the woman's comment. "What exactly am I looking for?" Abby asked.

"Anything out of place. It's a wedding. You know what they look like. Everyone thinks they are all different, that theirs is unique, but most of them are so similar. A professional like you will see something out of kilter."

"You mean like this woman bringing this guy to the church? Who is she?" Abby turned the screen for Gretchen's viewing.

"Olivia Stanton, Marty's wife. I knew it. She's wearing that shade of lipstick, and she's carrying two Waterford crystal flutes." Gretchen pointed at the screen. He is Trent Hampton, the groom. He's carrying an open bottle of champagne."

Abby turned the screen back without showing any emotion. "She is cozy with that young man. So, when did he die?"

"Within twenty to thirty minutes after he goes into the room at the rear of the church, with her."

"I'll keep watching." Abby was laser focused on the screen, especially after she noticed the added concern on the usually cool coordinator's face.

Gretchen left Abby alone and soon returned with two glasses of wine. "Here, cabernet, right?"

Abby nodded as she continued her search. She grabbed the glass, never missing a piece of film. She hit the stop key. "Gretchen, did you see that the bride went into that room a few minutes after that lady and the groom?"

"Really? I'm going to visit her tomorrow to pay my respects. She didn't tell anyone she went to see Trent. Instead, I heard she was a crying maniac after the discovery of the groom's body, telling everyone her entire life was over."

Abby began the film again as she took another sip of wine. She quickly placed the glass back on the table. "Gretchen, look. There's another man headed to the room." She pointed to the screen. "I'm not sure the video guy even knew what he was filming. He was probably shooting the arriving guests. There's a shot of the steeple--"

"What the blue blazes are you talking about?" Gretchen stood behind Abby.

"Here, look. He's about the groom's age. Now, let's see what happens." Abby began the film. "Look at that. He waits until the bride leaves before he goes in. That room was crowded. It must've been a real party. Now, the other young man comes out with the older woman. Yikes, he seems mad. Now, they're going back in. I can't see his face."

"They should've had a revolving door installed in that room just for that wedding. Keep looking, Abs. This is life and death, my life and Trent's death."

The two women continued to watch the screen. No one ever came out of the room. The next item of interest was Gretchen herself walking toward the back of the church, and into the room.

Abby's hands flew up. "Where did they go? There was no one in there with the groom when you arrived, was there?"

"No," Gretchen answered slowly. Her brain was working in overdrive. She needed to visit the bride. She needed to visit with the Hamptons, if they would allow her in the house. She needed to find out what was written on that note Delbert Hampton removed from his son's body. And she needed to give the police her other discovered piece of evidence.

"Wait. They could've gone out the back door on the other side of the church, or maybe they just went into the church and sat down. No one would've thought anything of that."

"Holy Moly," Abby muttered. Her boss always said that, and it seemed to serve as the decent exclamation for so many problems. "Lily and I would use that path so the guests wouldn't see us."

"Holy Moly indeed," Gretchen repeated. "Who would want to frame me for murder? I can't think of anyone who doesn't like me."

Abby drank the remainder of the liquid in her glass. She crossed her eyes. "Don't you? You can be a bit too much."

Gretchen pursed her lips as though she was ready to unload on her young friend. Instead, she laughed as she looked down at Abby. "Well, what's the point of living if you are just okay? There is never too much, too much excitement, adventure, money, nor me!"

Abby suspected that Gretchen's bravado was the mask for her fear. She had a right to be afraid. It did indeed look as though someone was framing the planner for a murder she didn't, nor could she, commit. Gretchen was a lot of things, but she wasn't a murderer. On a bad day, when Gretchen was demanding a single bloom be replaced, or yelling at the photographer for wearing khakis, one could contemplate throttling her from the top of her sprayed hair to the bottom of her high heels.

"Gretchen, what do you want me to do?" Abby sincerely wanted to help. She suspected no one else would. "What can I do for you?"

"I want you to look over the remainder of that film, and please take a look at the photographer's file. Maybe he has some shots of the inside of the church. I'm calling my attorney to find out how the groom was really killed. I've heard it was poison, but I need to know more. You just keep watching. I'm ordering Chinese. Aren't you a sweet and sour girl?"

Abby nodded. "Shrimp, please, as long as you are paying?"

"Of course. We are going to work all night until I'm vindicated."

Abby hit her head with her palm. All night with Gretchen might be the death of her. Or there might be another murder...

Chapter Nine

Wearing her favorite pair of red-bottom stilettos, Gretchen Malloy readied for battle. From head to toe she was dressed in designer threads, professional in a magnificent pants and blazer ensemble accented with large gold earrings, necklace, and her signature cuff bracelet. She wore her expensive watch on her other wrist and several thin diamond tennis bracelets. She was ready to fight and dressed to kill.

Leslie Bagby Underwood was happy to sit down and talk to her former wedding coordinator. By now her last name should be Hampton, but instead she would be attending Trent's funeral at the end of the week. She poured an iced tea for Gretchen and poured a scotch for herself.

"It's so nice to speak to someone who isn't telling me how sorry they are for me." The young woman sat across from her visitor. She was smiling and casual in a sleeveless romper. The large six-carat brilliant cut engagement ring was absent from her finger. "It's good to be free."

"I did want to check on you, but I had a few questions." Gretchen had no time for chit-chat, besides the twenty-something almost bride didn't appear to be grieving the passing of her almost husband.

"Sure, whatever you need." Leslie slumped back in the over-sized chair.

"I saw you visited with Trent before the wedding. What was all that about?" Gretchen's question made the girl sit up straight.

"You saw that?"

"Yes," Gretchen lied. "I also heard part of the conversation." *It is time to take a chance.* "Why did you scream at him?"

"Wouldn't you? I mean, I knew he cheated on me. I knew he really didn't want to get married, but you know our parents. We were the perfect couple of the season. We would be set with the money they were throwing at us. I thought marriage alliances died with Henry the VIII, but not with this crowd." She swept her hand around the room toward many family photos. "Did you know my mother and father married to join two financial institutions so the banks didn't fail?"

"Yes, I did. Leslie, it's a shame that you felt pressured. When you marry someone, you marry into a family, into a country club, into a life much like yours, but so different too." Gretchen knew those stories. Many times, society couples married their acquaintances. They were familiar, they were country club members. It was natural even though most people would cringe, but most people married those in their circles. But Chance and she hadn't worked.

"I was fine with Trent going away and having a good night, but I didn't want to hear about anything he would do in this city. He could go to Acapulco for a fling, or Vegas to watch strippers, but I wouldn't tolerate it here in our home."

Gretchen nodded in feigned understanding. "I totally agree with you. Did you need to warn him one more time before the marriage?"

"No, I told him the wedding was off."

Leslie's bluntness created a vacuum in the room, one filled with complete shock. Gretchen couldn't believe her ears. "But you had those photos with your bridesmaids and your parents. Why did you do that if the wedding was off?"

"To have some new pics with my girls and family. Didn't you notice who was missing? You seem to know everything."

Gretchen sat silently, picturing every moment of that day. She remembered the video and the photos. *Of course!* "Your maid of honor. I thought she was running late."

"No. I called her that morning and told her not to show up. Being the little witch that she is, she did come, but I didn't allow her in the photos. I held my tongue. I was going to walk up that aisle, go to that podium, and I was going to tell everyone about her. I was going to say that he needed to go home with the woman he slept with after our rehearsal dinner. It was my maid of honor. Then in complete dramatic fashion, I would glare at him, throw the bouquet at him or her, whoever I could target, and walk back down that aisle a free woman. The embarrassment factor would be my security that no one would or could convince me out of my decision. My parents couldn't tell me who to marry after a fiasco like that."

Leslie moved closer to the bottle of scotch on the table in front of her, pouring another full glass of liquor. "I can't wait to see who shows up at his funeral. I'll be watching for the criers and the moaners. If someone uses more than one tissue, I'll know. Seriously, if he was doing it with my best friend, and I know of at least six others over the course of our engagement, then I might be losing a few more friends."

Gretchen was usually poised for just about any situation, but now she had to add another name to the suspects' list, if not several more. It was crowded in that small room where Trent's dead body had been found. "Your maid of honor, wasn't that Lawrence Foster's daughter, Tracy?"

"Yes. I will ruin her, and I'll ruin the others if I see them at the funeral. Tracy explained they had a little too much to drink, and then she said Trent had been with someone else that night. At first, she thought it was you because it was an old lady."

Gretchen blinked once and stared into the young woman's eyes. "It wasn't me."

"Oh, I know. This woman was younger than you, and she wore that new Italian fragrance. You only wear American designers from your clothes to your scent."

Gretchen had to hand it to her. Leslie knew her perfumes. "It's my casual scent. I'll definitely wear a good French one for formal occasions," Gretchen admitted. *But Olivia wears the fragrance I smelled in the air and on the boy's jacket.* "By the way, how and when did Tracy leave? Did she visit Trent too?"

"She tried to, but he wasn't there. At least that's what she said. Tracy left through the door on the south side of the church, near where we were all dressing. I pushed her out of the dressing room. My father escorted her back to her car. While I went to tell him off, I saw her pull away."

Gretchen calculated the timing. She pictured a timeline in her head. She realized this was the church that Lily and Abby called "the church of many doors and locks" because of the many entrances and exits. *Of course, not everyone would park in the lot! They could and would park on the side where the bride's room was, where there was easy access to the side door of the church and to the sidewalk. Those paths led into the driveway and foyer. Abby was right. There was more than one way to get in and out of that church and have no one see you coming or going. When the church was open, not one of the doors had an alarm either.*

"Leslie, my dear Leslie, I am so sorry for everything you are going through. You are so courageous. You will find someone." Gretchen thought her consolation would be appreciated, but the almost bride began to sob.

"But I want Trent. I loved him so much."

Gretchen didn't smile, nor laugh. She didn't comment or comfort. *Women are so fickle. Women can be so difficult to read especially when they are performing, even to an audience of one. Thank the heavens I'm a woman unlike others.* "Of course you did, dear. I know it is hard to hear right now, but it will get easier. You are probably still in shock. Leslie, do you think you could answer one other little question for me?"

And with that, the tears dried up. "What?"

"Did Trent have you sign a prenup?"

Leslie drained her glass and laughed. "Are you kidding? He was supposed to sign my prenup, but that jerk still had it in his pocket, along with a check my father gave him the night before the wedding. I told him to destroy both of them, but he wouldn't. He said I would have to pay to call off the wedding. He didn't want to be embarrassed. Well, he should have thought about that before he took a dive with my friend, and then that other woman. Who does that the night before they are getting married?"

Gretchen stood up slowly, moving over to hug the woman. "I am so sorry to have brought back such awful memories, but I'm fighting for my career, Leslie. If you think of anything else, will you contact me?"

Leslie returned the hug. "Of course. You were the only right thing about my wedding, well except your heels. They make entirely too much noise." Leslie pointed down at the coordinator's signature shoes. "Oh, I just remembered. There were a pair of stilettos on the table next to two champagne glasses in that room when I barged in. Trent was shoving his shirt quickly into his unzipped pants. I wonder if a woman was hiding when I came in so unexpectedly?"

You think? What a little ninny! Olivia was probably hiding behind the cabinet, the same piece of furniture that Gretchen had landed next to that day. She looked down at the time on her watch. She needed to stop by the Hamptons, and the day was passing by too quickly. First, she would drop by Lily's to get a bouquet from Abby. Flowers would be a nice touch. Perhaps she could hide behind them so the grieving parents wouldn't notice her until she was admitted inside the home?

After a little lunch, grabbing the bouquet, and arriving at the Hamptons, Gretchen sat in her car parked in front of their expansive home in Johnson County. There were at least eight other vehicles lined up in the driveway, most likely other mourners comforting the couple. Gretchen took in a rather large breath of air and headed toward the door.

"Do you really think they will want to speak to you, Ms. Malloy?" It was a familiar voice, one she was surprised to hear, one that made her turn too quickly on her heels. She uttered a profanity as she nearly toppled over.

Detective Williams grinned from ear to ear at her loss of balance and more from her loss of control. He wondered how the woman wore those stilts. "I'm not sure you are going to be able to hide behind those flowers either."

"Well, aren't you the smarty. I wanted to offer my condolences. I haven't seen them since that day. Why, Detective Williams, I believe that was the same day we met for the first time."

Williams immediately lost his smile. The woman was infuriating. He knew she had no reason to murder the boy, but he sure wanted to jail her for some reason. Any reason would do, perhaps wearing stilettos after forty? He looked her up and down. She was an attractive woman with curves that could wreck a race car. He could see the years on her too. She hid them well, but here and there you could see the cracks in her armor. He decided then and there that he might try to be nice to her for just a few minutes. Besides, he was thinking about her way too often to suit him.

As he walked to her side, he grabbed her arm to prop her next to him. "We will go in together. They won't throw you out if you're with me."

"They might throw us both out, and then where will we be? Perhaps drinks on some Plaza patio? Or what about a lovely little bistro table rendezvous at a hotel rooftop bar? I'll even allow you to pay."

Williams chose to ignore everything she was saying, but a drink did sound good, and spending time with her might be an experience. But he was working. She did give him a headache every time he saw her. He shook his head and hit the doorbell without looking at his new partner. In a matter of seconds, a butler gave them access and guided them to a large living area that had been converted over to accommodate guests. There was a full cold buffet and a bar set up in the corner of the room.

Gretchen handed the flowers to the attending butler and began to head to the bar, but Williams pulled her back. "Oh no you don't. You are with me, and that's where you will be staying."

Gretchen batted her eyelashes. "Why Detective Williams, I didn't realize you were the jealous type. You just can't be without me, can you?"

His glare was his only answer to her. He saw the Hamptons sitting on a couch by the pool. The couple held hands while visiting with another couple. "You say nothing. Do you hear me?" Williams pointed only a couple of inches from Gretchen's face.

She nodded. "Well, do you understand?" he questioned. Gretchen nodded again. "Why won't you say something?"

"You said not to say anything, so I'm not." She wanted to stick her tongue out at his impudent face, his lovely little face, but she took the high road.

Detective Williams uttered some expletive and made a noise similar to that of a wounded bear, if one had ever heard a wounded bear. He pulled her along until they stood next to the Hamptons.

Immediately, the shouting began. "What is that woman doing here? She killed our son, our little boy," Rhonda Hampton screamed as she pointed in Gretchen's direction.

The detective raised his hands in the air as though he were attempting to calm her down. "Mrs. Hampton, Ms. Malloy wanted to pay her respects. Frankly, I believe Ms. Malloy did not kill your son. That's why I'm here. I need to talk to you both, privately would be preferable."

My, the detective could be very smooth. The woman immediately shut her mouth and looked over to her husband for his answer.

"We can go into my office. It's right over here," Hampton offered.

Williams and Gretchen followed the couple into a stand-alone building similar to a mother-in-law's guest house. Delbert Hampton sat behind his large mahogany desk as his wife took her position in the window seat, as far away from Gretchen as possible. The two visitors sat in the chairs in front of the desk.

Gretchen, since she had to be silent, perused the walls and all of the photos hanging. Delbert had a very colorful career, one in which he mingled with mayors and marketing executives, presidents and players, actors, and well, as Gretchen surveyed, a lot of asses. Delbert wasn't immune from getting his hands dirty. There had been a share of rumors and scandals involving so many of his business projects. The death of his son was just one more in a long line of front-page news stories that had ended badly for the man. *In all of those times, his reputation was kept intact. Maybe I will survive this?*

"Mr. Hampton, was your son on antidepressants?"

Gretchen whipped her head to the side to look at her companion. *He certainly knows how to make an entrance!*

"Yes, sometimes, my wife too, if that is your next question."

The detective pulled out a pad of paper and began to write. "Was there enough in the house at any one time to be used for an overdose?"

Hampton didn't even flinch. "Yes, I suppose so, but my son did not kill himself. That woman murdered him." The groom's father looked as though he would reach across the desk and strangle Gretchen on the spot.

Gretchen squirmed in her chair. She needed to ask a question, but she looked more like she needed to find the nearest bathroom. She patted her partner's sleeve, but he ignored her. She needed his attention. *What can I do?* Her hand slowly rose up. She motioned it in front of William's face as though she was a schoolgirl attempting to gain the teacher's attention to use the restroom.

Williams grimaced. "What? What is it, Ms. Malloy?"

"I didn't kill anyone." She gazed at Hampton and cleared her throat. "Could you tell us about the prenup?"

Williams held his face in place. His poker face was perfect, although he wanted to shake the woman next to him. "Mr. Hampton? Do you have a copy of the document?"

Gretchen held Hampton's cold stare. She wouldn't back down with her life on the line. "No, I do not."

"That's a lie," she muttered. "You took it out of his

pocket that day, along with a check." Williams turned to face her. "What? I just remembered that the paper looked like there was a check attached to it."

"Are you sure?" he whispered.

"Yes."

"Mr. Hampton, I'd like to see the prenup, and the check you removed from your son's pocket. Now."

Williams' demanding tone, sent a shiver down Gretchen's spine. The detective could scare a suspect with that voice, but not her. She wasn't a suspect, and she knew that now. There was a line forming to the right of the crowd who could've killed Trent.

Hampton turned in his chair and opened a secret compartment within the bookcase behind him. A drawer popped out. He pulled out the contract and the check, handing it over to the detective. "This is private. It really is none of your business."

Detective Williams shook the items at the couple. "This is evidence in a murder case of your own son. What am I going to find out, Mr. Hampton?"

The silence was unbearable as the four humans waited for something. Gretchen couldn't stand it any longer. She was not meant to be quiet. Her hand raised once more. Williams nodded.

"You might as well go ahead and say what you want, Ms. Malloy." Gretchen knew sarcasm and defeat when she heard it.

"You are going to discover that the Hamptons needed money. Leslie was calling the wedding and whatever financial deal off. The check was written out the night before by her father. That prenup probably detailed a delicious deal for the Hamptons from the Underwoods. Maybe it said something about philandering, and what they could lose if Trent got out of line and cheated?"

The silence from the other side of the room was broken as Rhonda lunged to violently strike out at Gretchen. "You need to shut your mouth. How dare you talk about my son in that manner."

"But you knew he was cheating on Leslie," Gretchen blurted out. "Trent cheated that day at the church."

Delbert Hampton rushed to hold his wife back as she attacked.

Gretchen moved her chair a few inches away from Rhonda's nails. "He was with the maid of honor after the rehearsal dinner, and with another woman the day of the wedding."

"Don't you think I know what my son did? He was a man. He liked women, and they pursued him. Why don't you tell the police about Olivia? She was constantly pushing herself on him." Rhonda snarled. "Is it because she's married to an old family friend, Ms. Malloy?"

Before Gretchen could answer, Detective Williams stood up. In one swift movement, he pushed Rhonda back into her seat. He pointed his finger at her as though she were a pet. "Stay. We will be talking to Mrs. Stanton, and now I suppose I'll be visiting the maid of honor as well. Any other secrets you two wish to reveal? Now is your time. The next time I find out that you have lied to me, or haven't been forthcoming, you will find yourself in cuffs for obstruction in a police investigation. I won't mess around with this even if it is the murder of your son."

My, my, my. Detective Williams could definitely be the strong but silent type. He isn't just a man with pretty eyes. He headed to the door, and Gretchen followed obediently. In an instant, he became a man she would gladly follow.

"One more thing," Williams said in true Columbo fashion. "Did Trent have any medical issues?"

"No, not anymore," his mother answered. "When he was a child, he had an autoimmune flare up that almost cost him his life. He had a fatty liver, but he has been in the picture of health since then."

Gretchen tugged on the detective's sleeve. For some reason he looked up to the ceiling before answering her. "What, Ms. Malloy? What in heaven's name do you need?"

Gretchen winked at him and added a coy smile. "Well, why did he wear a medical alert bracelet?"

Instead of pushing Gretchen out of the door or yelling at the top of his lungs, Williams remained stoic. "Mrs. Hampton, why? Why did he wear a bracelet?"

Rhonda's eyes narrowed into tiny slits of hatred. "Apparently, Ms. Malloy knows everything, or wants to know everything. I don't know why that is important, but if you must know it was a simple allergy to peanuts, but he could become deathly ill."

Gretchen thought before she spoke this time. "Did he wear the bracelet the day of the wedding, Rhonda?" Her softer tone was answered with a nod.

"Of course. We had a new caterer for the engagement

party last year, and they had a passed appetizer. The dish had merely been set out next to a garnish of nuts. Trent ate one, and we had to call the paramedics."

"Didn't he have an EpiPen?" Gretchen questioned while Williams stood back.

Rhonda Hampton began to sob the very real tears of a mourning mother. "The boy always was misplacing the darn thing, and we didn't have any in reserve at our house. He'd moved to his apartment the year before. We almost lost him that day."

Williams began to walk away, but Gretchen pulled him back. She took a few steps over to the mother who had lost a son. Gretchen sat down next to her and placed her arm around her shoulders. "Rhonda, did all of his friends know about the allergy?"

"Yes, in fact they were all very protective of him. Most of the boys knew about his childhood problems too. All of them had been in school together, even Olivia's boys."

Gretchen nodded knowingly. "Are you telling me that Olivia's sons were in grade school with Trent?"

Rhonda wiped at her eyes. "Yes. Olivia and her first husband lived here when the boys were young. They moved to the New York area when Trent was in fourth grade. They all reconnected in college. Ryan, that campaign manager knew them too."

Alarms, whistles, bells, and everything else that made noise was going off in Gretchen's head. *They are all connected. My, the list just keeps getting longer.*

"Ms. Malloy, we really should be going." Williams watched as Gretchen Malloy kissed the mourning mother on the cheek and the two women swore they would have lunch at the club after all of this was over. Once Gretchen was at his side, he clutched her shoulders and pushed her out to the pool area.

"I really don't want to admit it, but you were brilliant in there," Williams murmured so only his companion could hear. "Too bad you didn't ask her about any reaction to alcohol."

Gretchen laughed out loud. "That's an obvious answer. If the boy had liver problems when he was little, alcohol could be a trigger. I met with the couple a few times. Once we had lunch. He declined a beer. I noticed he had snacks in his pocket at the rehearsal."

"You do notice things, don't you?" Williams shook his head as he placed his hand on Gretchen's back. They made their way through the throng of sympathizers who had gathered in the large living area. A few mourners shot glances at the woman they thought was a murderer. "Trent was a Type-2 diabetic. What I don't understand is why he would drink two different kinds of alcohol right before his wedding if he had a compromised liver?"

"I'd say he drank with two different people," Gretchen answered. "Oh, and he had been drinking quite a bit that week. His father and his mother thought he had passed out that day. I did too when I first came in the room."

"What? He drank with two different people?"

As she clicked her way along the wood floor through the house, Williams followed. Gretchen had a theory. He also knew she was keeping secrets from him.

"Olivia came in with two champagne flutes, and Trent

held the open bottle. When Olivia's son came in, I bet he had a flask on him. Those young men like their bourbon. That's what they were drinking at the rehearsal dinner."

Williams marveled at her. Of course, she was right. Trent's clothing reeked from the smell of bourbon, and the glasses had held very expensive champagne. From the video shot from the day of the wedding, Williams already knew that Trent had the open bottle with him, and was accompanied by a woman. Apparently, Gretchen Malloy had seen the same film, or was just a very good investigator. After a visit to the Stantons, the detective noticed the glasses were from the collection held within the china cabinet. To finish off the deadly cocktail, the groom's stomach content held antidepressants along with peanut oil. Mixed together, and given his past health history, he would've been a dead man in less than thirty minutes. Perhaps, he had taken a few pills before he came to the church too, not realizing that someone was going to poison him. Ms. Malloy was being framed by someone in the Stanton household. He knew that for sure. He could think of a thousand reasons why someone would want to derail the life of the most obnoxious, irrational, and controlling woman he'd met in a very long time.

"I need to give you something now that I'm not a suspect."

Williams looked up from his thoughts. "I never said you were off the hook."

Gretchen opened her car door and placed her purse on the seat. She began to rifle through it. "Yes, you did. Besides, you know I didn't do it. You are an intelligent man, and not just a pretty face."

His head was throbbing. "Your shoe had blood on it, and there were marks on his neck. Who would do that after someone was dead?"

Completely disregarding his statement about the stiletto wounds on a dead body, Gretchen continued her search. *I absolutely hate it when I switch to a larger bag, and I can never find anything. It all goes to the bottom, including my valuable evidence.* She dug deeper and fished the item out. "There it is. You'll need this before you talk to Olivia."

Williams' eyes widened at her discovery contained in a small plastic bag. "What the hell?"

"You're a bright man. Safety first and all. It's a condom with pink lipstick on it. It will match the shade found on the champagne flutes. And, if you look closely within our little safety wrapper, you'll find a small link from Trent's medical emergency bracelet."

He looked at the item. He examined it closely and looked up at his companion. Somehow, and for no apparent obvious reason, her knowing smile didn't bother him this time. "When did you find this, and where?"

"I kept it as insurance so I wasn't railroaded to the big house."

"Could you sound more like an old movie?"

"Do you like old movies too? What about *It Happened One Night*? It is my favorite, well anything with Clark Gable or Cary Grant is swell with me. You're probably more of a Gary Cooper man, or maybe Bogart?"

"Swell," Williams repeated and grinned. Her features had softened as she talked about those old film actors. She was, well, very attractive. He shook it off. "Where, and when did you get this?"

"It was in the garbage bin the night you arrested me for the second time," Gretchen laughed. "This is like that old game...Gretchen in the garbage with a flashlight picking up glasses and a condom. That beats Colonel Mustard in the library with a candlestick any day."

He examined the evidence again and saw the link clearly. Apparently, the bracelet was pulled off of him in some sort of struggle. "What you just said is so wrong. You need to promise me you won't talk to your friends the Stantons about all of this."

Gretchen stopped smiling. Their brief interlude was over, and he was all business once more. "I promise I won't, besides Olivia doesn't really talk with me. She talks at me. Marty is my friend."

"And he is launching his campaign in a week or two?"

Gretchen nodded. "I don't need to see them until the day of the event. I can do all my work from my home."

"Good. For your safety, I'll have an officer stop in now and then."

Her clapping took him by surprise. "I do love a man in uniform. Well, actually, I like a man out of uniform too." Gretchen's giggle seemed to offend the man.

Williams' headache was beyond treatment. He remained silent. He walked back to his car and waited for her to pull away. He decided he would follow her back to the apartment, just in case. Someone was truly framing Gretchen Malloy. Now, it would take so little to determine who and why.

"She likes a man out of uniform too." The detective began to laugh until tears came to his eyes. Suddenly, his headache vanished.

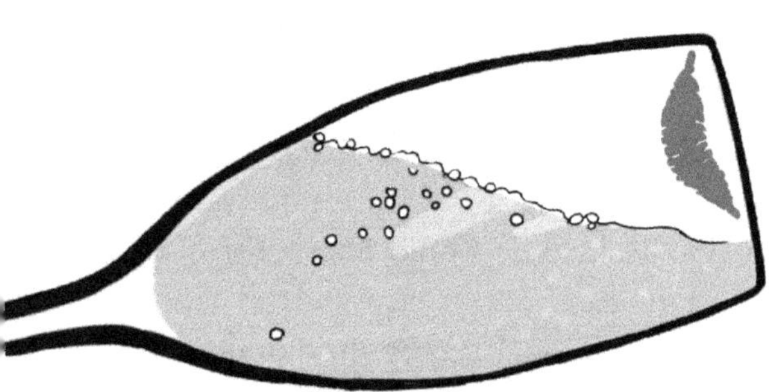

Chapter Ten

"What did you do?" Chance Alexander stormed into Gretchen's apartment in a sizzling rage. His face was red, and it wasn't from the rising temperatures outside in humid Kansas City.

"It's nice to see you too, Chance." Gretchen had no clue why her former love was in such a mood. *Had he missed his daily showing of Perry Mason? He used to love that program.* Years ago, she would pretend to watch while she studied. As long as they were sitting next to each other in that awful apartment they had shared, she was happy. Simple things used to make her so content.

"Olivia is upset. Marty is upset. He is questioning the entire campaign now. I don't care if he runs or not, but I do care if he gets hurt."

Chance quickly made his way to the living area and sat down on the sofa as though he was completely at home. Gretchen liked how he looked sitting in her apartment. He looked like he should be there as a permanent fixture. He could be the most handsome accessory at home, much like her favorite toss pillow. When they left the apartment, she would adorn his arm like a comfortable leather jacket. He was everything she always had wanted, well, except for that temper. That, she could do without. But she never wanted him to lose his admirable loyalty to his love and his friends.

"I care if Marty gets hurt too. I really don't care what happens to Olivia." Gretchen's admission was without any emotion. She knew she had the truth on her side. "Because of Marty, I held back evidence from the police until the other day. Because of Marty, I accessed the photos and video from the wedding in an attempt to hope that I was wrong about the lipstick on the toasting flutes. Because of Marty, I may have sacrificed my career so that he can have his dream."

"You don't think about anyone but yourself."

Gretchen casually strode over to her liquor cabinet. She poured a glass of vodka and threw it down her throat. When she turned to him, she was ready.

"Don't you dare tell me I don't care. You, of all people, know better."

Chance hung his head in despair. He did know better. In college she had worked two jobs while going to classes just so he didn't have to work with his heavy class load during his last semester. She would've done anything for him back then. Apparently, Gretchen had stayed in touch with Marty even after Amy's death. She connected with him by note or phone several times a year. Marty had recounted those sad days to Chase, and explained how Gretchen had single-handedly kept them all alive even though she was hurting just as much as the rest.

"I'm sorry. I just don't know what to do."

Gretchen pulled back her hair over her ear and tilted her head.

"What did you say? I didn't hear you? Were you speaking some foreign language?"

As she poured herself another vodka, and poured bourbon into another one for her guest, Chance repeated his apology. "I said I was sorry. I'm so sorry."

Gretchen placed the glass on the table in front of him. "Still bourbon neat, right?"

"Yes." He pointed at her drink. "Vodka, right?"

"Yes. I was just about to order dinner."

His lips formed a slight smile. "You're not cooking tonight, great chef?"

"You know damn well I'm not. I have a restaurant on speed dial that will deliver the perfect steak. Are you in?"

Chance nodded. "I'd like that very much. I think we need to talk."

Through dinner, they kept their conversation to mundane subjects. Gretchen recounted several obscenely funny wedding stories, and Chance talked about some of his non-secret government jobs. They laughed and enjoyed the meal. Afterward, they moved out to the balcony with a couple cups of coffee and one piece of cheesecake.

"Taste this. It is the best cheesecake," Gretchen said as she placed a full fork near her guest's mouth. Chance gladly accepted the bite of dessert.

"My, oh my, that is good. Where did you get that from?"

"I baked it." She took a bite and relished the taste.

"I don't believe it." Chance watched her. "You don't cook, but you bake? The world is coming to an end."

Gretchen smirked at his attempt at humor. "I can cook. I choose not to. I could always bake, and cheesecake is my specialty. I've developed this recipe over the years. It's based on one of my mother's."

Chance took a sip of coffee. The sun was near to setting, but was providing a sky of purples, pinks and even touches of gold. It was a magnificent backdrop for the Plaza with its tremendous architecture of towers and clay roofs.

"Your mom was a great cook. I still dream about her pot roast and that strawberry pie."

"If you stick around for more than a few weeks, I'll make your dream come true and fix it for you. I have the recipe."

Chance touched her hand softly and looked into her eyes. She wasn't wearing those silly fake eyelashes tonight. She looked like his G rather than a racoon. "I wish I could stay. As soon as Marty announces, I have a group taking over while I head to Virginia Beach and to that new grandchild."

Gretchen nodded. *What possessed me to make that suggestion to him?* These weren't old feelings returning to the surface. They were the same ones she lived with all of her life. She had made a decision and so did he. Those choices changed a lifetime for them. "That is going to be one loved baby. I'm so happy for you." She smiled as sweetly as she could. She wanted to cry, but she wouldn't. At least that's what she told herself.

"But I'll probably be back. Marty will be traveling around the state, and I'll be at his side. I'll count on that roast. Gretchen, I'd like to stay in touch this time."

"This time," Gretchen murmured. She placed her fork down and faced him. "Chance, the police don't want me talking to Marty or to Olivia. I can continue working on the event, and of course I'll be there to make sure everything runs smoothly, but I can't talk to them about that murder."

Chance drew back his hand. "The detective was at the house asking questions. Apparently, Olivia was having an affair with that young man. Marty didn't have a clue. He was devastated. I gather the murder victim was a friend of Olivia's oldest son, BJ. They found two glasses, and one had Olivia's lipstick on it. On top of it, they found a used condom, and it had her lipstick on it too."

There was no need to be open with Chance about her part in the acquisition of that evidence, nor how she had acquired it. She was finally feeling clean again. Gretchen caught her friend's hand in hers. "What is Marty going to do?"

"He's going through with the announcement. He moved into the other side of the house for now. It feels like a freezer in there. I don't know how to fix this."

"Chance, you can't fix this. This is serious. Just because Olivia had a fling doesn't mean she is a murderer, no more than I am."

"Why did they think you had something to do with it?"

"Now, there's a story!" Gretchen glanced at the beautiful sky and took a breath. "Look at that."

"It's lovely, but still not as pretty as the sun over the ocean, remember?"

We used to walk hand-in-hand to see the sunset on the beach. We used to stay in each other's arms until it was pitch black. How could she forget? "Yes. Those were some lovely days."

"And nights," Chance added. "By the way, you look absolutely stunning tonight."

She shoved his arm, his very muscular arm. "I haven't done my hair, I have very little makeup on, no lipstick, no jewelry, no designer clothes, and I'm barefoot."

"I like those feet way more than those stilettos. Put them up here, and I'll give them a good rub. You always liked that."

Gretchen didn't even stop to think or to question her actions. Chance moved back his chair, and she lifted her feet into his lap. She hadn't had her feet rubbed by a man since--since Chance used to do it.

"Chance, did the police tell you that someone was trying to frame me for that murder?"

Chance's attention was on her feet and his mission to give her the best foot rub. "That detective mentioned something to me. He didn't go into detail."

"Someone punctured the boy's neck with a stiletto."

Chance's head flew up. "What? Who would do that?"

"Someone who wanted me out of the way. Perhaps that person was scared that I was more than just an old friend. Maybe that person was trying to cover up the fact that she was having an affair with the young man who had just been killed."

She expected him to go into a flying rage, but instead he went back to her feet. "Olivia? I figured. She's been concerned about Marty's affection toward you. He tapped it down and told me he thought it was a bit of insecurity or jealousy on her part. She's more comfortable in New York, not here in Kansas City."

Gretchen believed that insecurity was a weakness, and she very rarely allowed herself to wallow in it. There were times when the feeling would creep in, usually when she was feeling lonely and had no one to turn to. She was never the type of woman to have girlfriends, but just in the last couple of years she had made a best friend in Lily, and now in Abby. Even though they were younger than her, they tolerated her outlandish and sometimes pretentious behavior. *I know what kind of person I am, but I enjoy every minute of being who I am.*

"And where are you comfortable, Chance?" *Where did that question come from?* Chance always created an awkward vulnerability for her when he touched her in any way. It was his superpower.

He pulled her chair closer to him; her legs bent. "I am right now with you."

"Anywhere else?" Her voice was soft and lingered on the air.

"I can think of one other place, but it would still be with you."

"Tell me about it."

He slid her legs off of his lap and stood up. His hand beckoned to her. "I'd rather take you there and show you." He lifted her up until she stood in his arms.

"The bedroom is in there." She pointed inside. Her heart was beating faster again. It had its own tune. It was a familiar, old, romantic song that meant everything to her.

Chance placed his hands on either side of her face and kissed her softly on each cheek and then lightly on her lips. "I want to stay the night in your arms. Please let me."

Gretchen locked her arms around his neck and pushed into the kiss until they both broke apart breathlessly.

"I could never say no to you."

Chance's eyelids dropped to shield the hurt. "You did one time, that last time."

"You were going away with the Marines. Yes, I said no. You didn't ask me. You told me."

He kissed her solidly again. "I don't want to go back there again, do you?"

Chance wondered if she'd allow the past to ruin tonight when Gretchen left his arms. Instead, she pulled him into the apartment and toward the bedroom. The room was an obvious mirror of its owner featuring a gold and silver wallpaper pattern on three walls, and a black painted one behind the king-sized bed layered with silver covers. Chance watched as Gretchen threw her multitude of decorative bed pillows onto the floor and threw back the bedspread as though she were flipping letters on a game show.

She walked seductively to him. As she began to unbutton his shirt, she trailed his chest with kisses. "You don't know how long I have waited to do this," she murmured.

"You mean, you've been thinking about me all this time?" His low chuckle seemed to spur her on as she pulled off his shirt.

Her eyes lingered on him and his broad, still muscled chest. "Yes, I have. I'm not embarrassed to admit it." Gretchen threw the shirt over a bedroom chair.

"As long as we are being honest, I have thought about you each and every day since I left you."

Gretchen pulled him close to her. "You should never have left me."

Chance's eyes narrowed. They could verbally battle all night or they could love each other. He gathered her face again in his large hands and drew her mouth to his. "I'm not going anywhere tonight."

Gretchen literally melted into his arms, her body weight completely buoyed by his body and molding her frame to his. He was still the young man she had fallen in love with, but now his maturity offered so much more. She ran her hands through his silver hair. She kissed his lips, his chin, his neck, and trailed down his bare chest. For his age, his body was in magnificent shape, but she noticed a scar or two that hadn't existed before. She ignored a Marine tattoo. "And I don't want you to leave."

As Gretchen unleashed his belt and began to unzip his pants, Chance chuckled. "I can tell, G. Slow down."

"It's been a long time for us. I don't want to waste one second before it's morning, and you leave me again."

He tipped her chin up. "But then I can keep coming back, if that's what you want. I have a feeling you would get tired of me if I was a permanent fixture."

Gretchen stepped out of his hold and surveyed his body. She nodded as if accepting the inevitable. She took his hand and led him to the bed. She lowered her body down slowly as though she was a precious piece of china worth the wait to receive as a gift. Her provocative behavior elicited only one response. "Then prove to me that you just aren't a pretty fixture."

For a brief second, Chance fought his heated feelings for her. They were always on fire for each other. Apparently that hadn't vanished with the years of separation.

"I always do like to make a good impression." He turned out the lamp at the side of her bed and joined her. Years and miles disappeared. It was only just the two of them until morning.

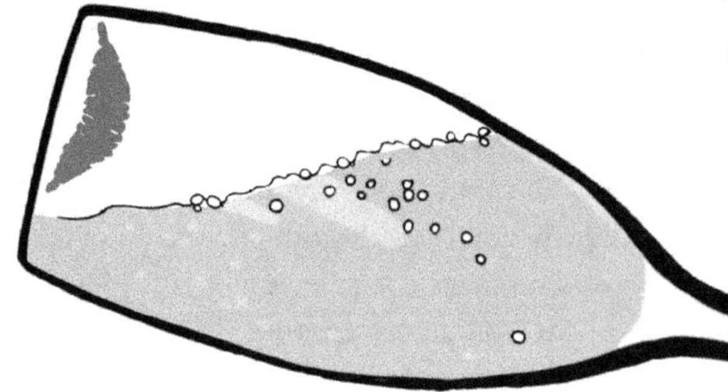

Chapter Eleven

Gretchen heard water running. She rolled over like she did every morning, alone. But in her bathroom was a divine man who was apparently showering. She looked at the clock and saw that it was nearly seven. Most mornings, she was making coffee and eating toast by now, but this morning she stared at her ceiling and smiled. Their fire hadn't been extinguished. They both were burning for each other, but that had never been their problem. *Holy Moly, I still love him.*

She grabbed the loose sheet around her and headed into the other room. In her head, she was giving gratitude to her contractor for suggesting the clear glass on the shower. Chance's form could be seen clearly.

"My, my, my." She was frozen. She looked upon those shoulders and that expanse of skin and muscle that she had used as a pillow, mesmerized by his form. *That body was always a problem.* She was always so easily dissuaded during a serious conversation by that man with those luscious lips that could perform such magical tricks on her own body.

The water stopped running, and Chance peeked his head out of the shower. "Some things never change, G."

"Me watching you?"

As he exited, he wrapped a towel around his lower half. "Nope." He reached over to her hanging silk stockings.

"You still wash out your hose and hang them, don't you?"

"I treat them nicely. They are of value."

He kissed her quickly on the lips. "Ah, I'm assuming I am valuable because I was surely treated nicely last night."

Chance combed his hair as Gretchen came up from behind him and hugged his chest. "And I was too. It was lovely."

He looked in the mirror at her unmade face, her hair mussed in every direction. "Now that we're older it seemed to mean so much more."

Gretchen pulled away. "It meant everything years ago. But time does change you. Thank you for your beautiful words about my body. I know it isn't like it used to be. Time does change your skin no matter how much I try to ignore it."

Chance saw the lament on her face and turned to gather her up in his arms, pulling the sheet away from her body in one swift move. "You are so much more beautiful in the morning when you are completely naked. There's no makeup, or extra lashes, no lipstick, or jewelry. And this hair--" Chance ran his hands through it, pulling it back from her face. "Look at you. You are amazing."

I won't survive this. At this rate, the man will give me a cardiac episode. Seriously, she couldn't stand to have her heart broken by him again. "I'm always amazing." Her tone was one she would use on the job at some wedding or charity event.

He kissed the top of her head. "I will never debate that. I've got to get to work." He reached down and handed her the sheet.

Gretchen wrapped up and kicked at the long length of Egyptian cotton as she shuffled into her closet. She had a short day with visits to the caterer, the sound system company, the photographer, and the videographer for the event. With the big day tomorrow, she would check in with the campaign manager by email and text to confirm timelines, and to extinguish any unexpected problems. She would text Marty and tell him all was good. She would honor her promise to the handsome detective and not call or drop by until tomorrow. Once the event began, she would be in her element and in charge. There wouldn't be anytime to discuss the murder or Olivia's involvement, but she did have something in mind. She was so good at discovering evidence she thought she might go looking for more while the party was going on. *Distraction could equal discovery!*

"What is that detective's first name?" Apparently Chase hadn't heard her question. *He's never told me his name. That's strange.* It wasn't necessary, but it would be nice to know. A first name would make him more human and less like a machine.

She selected a decade old French designer ensemble for the day and hung it on the door. She felt Chance watching her as he put on his shoes. He was dressed and ready to leave.

"I have no idea what his name is." Chance slipped on his jacket and straightened his sleeves. "I suppose I won't see you until the event tomorrow."

Gretchen nodded. "I'll be there early in the morning so would you make sure security knows? I'll be there no later than eight, and I'll need to park my car so I have access to the driveway just in case I have to leave to grab anything we may have forgotten. Usually, that doesn't happen, but I never believe that every risk has been covered completely."

Chance saluted. "Yes, ma'am. I will make sure security knows you are coming, and you will have access to your vehicle at all times. Now, I need to leave."

He took a few steps toward her. Gretchen knew that smoldering look in his eyes. She raised her hand to stop him. She promised herself she wouldn't be hurt again. Any love affair would always be on her terms, and it had been working very nicely that way since the day he had left her.

"Don't, just go. Don't say anything, or make any promises."

Chance Alexander felt her retreating, making her heart stop feeling. He understood. He could feel his heart slowing, hardening. "I was just going to kiss you, but I'll leave. I will see you tomorrow, G."

Before she could protest, which she would not do, Chance had let himself out. She sniffed back a tear, held her head up, and proceeded to take her own shower, completely alone. She never cried, but in the shower, how could one tell?

Chapter Twelve

By Saturday morning, Chance's scent was completely gone from her skin. She arrived at the Stanton Mansion a little before eight. One of Chance's team members directed her to the perfect parking space near the edge of the tennis courts. Her car would be only one of four on the driveway and easily accessible. The guests' vehicles would all be valet parked at a rented lot near the country club. The organized planner carried her bag with all her event notes, her designer purse, a small piece of rolling luggage, and a hanger bag containing her gown for the evening.

Directed to the massive utility room by the old butler's pantry, Gretchen made her own makeshift office laying out all of her information on the desk. The room was hers for the day. A door opened from one of the garages, and Chance entered her domain.

"Hello beautiful." His smile melted her cooling heart. "How can you just make me feel better by seeing you?"

"Don't you know it's my special loving powers?" She smiled sweetly, but her eyes glanced at her file folder. "I have to get to work, and I don't need any distractions. Do you need something from me?"

Chance's low laughter made her realize what suggestion the question had elicited.

"I could think of a few things, but we are both professionals."

"I could think of more than a few things, few of which are probably illegal in Missouri, but you are right. Today, we need to stay focused. Actually, we always have our jobs, don't we?" Her smile faded. Chance had his daughter, and soon he would have that little baby. *I have my life I've made in this city.*

"I'll let you get on with your work," Chance suggested. "If you do need me for any reason, just yell."

"I'd love one of those cool looking earpieces." She pointed toward his head.

"Those are just for the security staff. We'll hear everything, and have access to anything we need, including a helicopter if necessary. And you," Chance said as he pointed his finger at her, "stay out of trouble. If you do get in trouble, you yell. I mean it. Marty is my priority, but you are too. Never forget that."

As he passed her, he stopped quickly to break his own rules, to kiss her on the cheek. If they did have a chance at any future, he didn't want to be the one to mess things up, this time. As a remembered habit, Gretchen reached around to gently embrace him. It felt comfortable, and for Chance it gave him an opportunity to view the items she had brought in. Once Gretchen had left the room, he and another one of his men would search them. But Gretchen didn't need to know that. With that thought, he pulled away and gave her one more quick kiss. He had work to do.

And Gretchen did too. She showed the rental company where to place the podium, the tables, the chairs, and the bars. The sound professionals wired everything, and the system was working perfectly. Tablecloths were flying, glasses were being stacked, and Gretchen was in charge. She had no thoughts of Chance, Olivia, Marty, or any murder.

The busy coordinator took a short break around noon. The catering company swarmed the kitchen and provided her with a salad and a croissant. She made sure she rested and remembered to stay hydrated. Olivia, Marty, and Ryan were nowhere to be seen, but Olivia's sons were in Marty's office. They were clearly watching her as she added a few candles around the pool. She shook off their stares and kept her head down. *Momma always said to stay out of sight and out of mind.*

But Gretchen was watching. She didn't know what she was looking for, but somehow, she knew that somewhere in this house was the answer to solving a murder.

Around two in the afternoon, Abby and her friendly face arrived with the arrangements and the floating pool flowers. Two of her helpers headed into the house to decorate while Abby stripped off her jeans and shirt.

"What are you doing, young lady?" Gretchen yelled as she saw the clothing thrown off.

Under the clothes, Abby wore a black swimsuit. "I'm swimming, remember? I have to place the flowers in the pool."

Abby's very understated one-piece was suddenly understandable. "Oh, yes. Will you need any help?" Gretchen wouldn't mind a little soak in the pool in this warm weather even if it was just a little soak for her feet.

"Nope, I've got this, but if you could hang around so you can see if I have the flowers in the correct positions?"

"Of course, Abby." Gretchen could direct and surveille suspects at the same time. Currently, Abby prepared one of the pool arrangements for its big swim. Gretchen concentrated on Ryan Marley. He had finally arrived and was talking head-to-head with Olivia on the covered patio. *They certainly are a little too cozy for comfort. Why should a campaign manager and the candidate's wife be so close, so intimate with each other? He has his arm around her waist.* Gretchen began to walk toward them when she heard Abby.

"Wait." Abby's phone was ringing. "It's Lily."

Gretchen sighed. She really did miss her little bestie, but Lily was living a grand life with a loving man in Virginia. Her occasional visits back to Kansas City were always a highlight for Gretchen. *And there's always a void when she leaves me.*

"She's right here. Do you want to talk to her?" Abby handed the phone to the planner. "It's for you, Gretchen."

"Bestie," Gretchen said loudly as she held the phone up to her ear.

"I hear you have been involved in a murder. What did Dev and I tell you about spying on your own?"

Gretchen rolled her eyes. "You told me not to do it. Holy Moly. I want to know how Mr. Delicious is." She had called Lily's husband Devlin, Mr. Delicious from day one because, well, because he was!

"Don't use my phrase against me. Dev is fine. We're all fine, and we want you to be fine too. Don't get yourself in trouble, and don't get carried away with any infatuation that is going to hurt you."

How did Lily know? I'll just ignore her, and she won't be the wiser. "Abby is getting into the pool so I better go. I need to watch over her. She's just not you. Oh, she's very good, but she isn't Lily! I wish you were here to team up with me again. Pierce and Malloy could solve this."

"Gretchen, I'm not sure if you're talking about the flowers now or the mystery you've plunged yourself into, but either way let the professionals do their jobs," Lily reprimanded. "I mean it. Don't get into anything that is over your head. You aren't Jessica Fletcher! And we both know Abby is fantastic so cut her some slack."

Gretchen made a face. *Lily never used to speak back to me. I'm not sure I like this independent streak of hers.* Abby laughed as she watched the conversation. Only Lily, and sometimes she could, make Gretchen halfway human. "Lily, I know better. You're Jessica Fletcher, and I haven't decided who I am yet. I'm thinking I'm more like Mata Hari. I liked her style."

"And the heels?" Lily laughed.

"It's always the heels. Don't you ever forget that, darling."

Lily couldn't agree with Gretchen's fashion advice. "Those stilettos are your thing, everyone knows that. My speed is sneakers if I'm decorating a wedding or event, or maybe some stylish flats. Never those killers! But you never do anything halfway."

"Exactly," Gretchen muttered. Gretchen felt as though a lightbulb turned on over her head. Ironically, with the excitement of knowledge came calm.

Lily could barely hear her. "Gretchen?"

"Honey, I need to go. We are working here. My best to you all. I'll call you when all of this is over--"

"Gretchen? Don't you do anything stupid. I can hear it in your voice. Promise me."

"Dearie, I am never stupid. I may be obstinate, flamboyant, and irritating to some, but I'm never stupid. Seriously, I have to go. Tootles." Before Lily could admonish her comments, Gretchen pressed the red button to end the call. She headed to the edge of the pool near Abby who was already in the water with a large floating flower arrangement. "Now, let's go to work."

Abby saw something in Gretchen's eyes. Usually, she would say Gretchen was a little scarier, but knowing her now as she did, she knew it was Gretchen being Gretchen. But it seemed as though there was just a little too much glee in those eyes. Gretchen knew something, and Abby didn't want to know anything. Living in the dark had its perks and offered her a very limited view of a nasty world. Oblivion equaled happiness.

By almost six, most of the guests were mingling around the pool, enjoying the drinks and passed appetizers. Olivia was adorned in a short cocktail dress in the prettiest shade of azure blue. Her long legs were perfectly tanned; her heels were at least six inches high. On her ears, she wore a simple styled pair of pearls and diamonds, and around her neck her choker featured more diamonds than pearls. A large blue sapphire hung from it.

Gretchen spied Marty talking to his campaign manager. He was going over his script for the announcement just one more time. He looked up as if he felt her eyes on him and motioned her over. "Gretchen, I want to move my announcement back until after seven. I don't think the press will mind waiting if they are fed, do you?"

"No, that shouldn't be a problem. Is there a reason why you want to wait?" She would have to talk to the reporters and offer them some sort of an explanation to waste their time at a cocktail party.

"I don't need a reason, do I?" Marty's voice raised enough to have a couple of startled guests cease their conversations.

Gretchen smiled sweetly to convey all was well, but decidedly they were not. *Marty has never raised his voice, but he is under a lot of pressure.* She nodded her acceptance and understanding of the direct command. "Of course not. No problem. I'll inform the press unless Ryan would like to do it."

Ryan patted her on the back. "You know them. I would really appreciate it if you did it." Her skin crawled at his touch.

Now that she had her marching orders, Gretchen nodded once more and headed over to the press. But she noticed Ryan and Olivia glancing across the pool at each other. *If they can communicate like this with stolen glances, then they absolutely have something going on. Right now, I don't have the time to deal with them.* She pacified the reporters' questions and suggested the shrimp cocktail was one food they shouldn't miss. The crustaceans had been flown in from the Keys that morning.

Gretchen noticed that Lawrence Putnam, the political reporter for one of the news stations was missing.

"Where did that little guy go?" she muttered as she did a thorough survey of the crowd. She knew he liked to roam and left unattended in the house, who knew what he might get himself into. The man was a known sneak. Lately, he had become a snitch and a snake. He was desperate for a titillating story. But Gretchen could handle him and his little games.

Last year, Gretchen caught Putnam rifling through a woman's purse. He was searching for any bit of evidence to confirm an affair between the event's hostess and the honored businessman of the year. Gretchen smiled. She'd handled him in the appropriate manner. She had hit his hands and snapped the purse closed on his fingers.

"You just assaulted me," Putnam had yelled.

Gretchen had just laughed as she freed his hand. "You haven't seen assault, Lawrence. I'll ruin you if I find you doing anything out of line tonight. Do you understand me?"

The reporter had muttered.

"Mr. Putnam, do we have an understanding? I'd be more than happy to contact the police chief. He could send a little patrol car with a couple of officers--"

Putnam waved off his blackmailer. "Fine. Yes. We have an understanding, but you have to give me something, Gretchen. We've known each other for so long."

"Sometimes it seems too long," Gretchen admitted. She looped her arm in his and steered him back to the party. "Fine. Go over to John Palmer over there. He will be announcing his retirement, and you might as well cover the story."

Gretchen and the reporter had ended the night on the right foot, but Lawrence could always go out of step at any time. *I don't need him inserting himself in this mess and hurting Marty in the process.*

As Gretchen said hello to guests as she trailed into the house, Chance maintained a close distance. "Wait up, G." She slowed her pace.

"I'm looking for a reporter, Chance."

He caught up and grabbed her arm to pull her to face him. He needed to see her eyes. "You know something, don't you?"

"I know I need to find this reporter. I don't want him looking through the house. He's a little guy, about this high." She motioned with her hand at about five feet in height. "He's one of the most popular political reporters in Kansas City. He's also one of the most ruthless. I want him corralled and not snooping around."

Chance was suspicious of her explanation. She had this look. She wasn't lying, but she wasn't telling the truth either. Her eyes betrayed her. "Gretchen Florence Malloy, you need to tell me right now what you know."

She pulled her arm out of his grasp, cringing as he said her middle name. "For your information, I only use my middle initial. Stop saying that word, and you need to allow me to do my job. I know someone is trying to frame me. Everyone knows I wear heels, and that's why they left those marks on Trent's neck. Sure, many women do, but they knew I was the coordinator. I was going to be there and would be the perfect fall guy, well fall woman. Maybe it was a joke or even a warning. I don't know yet, but I do know there's a killer here at this party, and they want me to take the fall. I'm not going down so easily. I refuse to be led away to the big house."

"But if you need me--"

"I don't need anyone." Gretchen regretted the sentence as soon as the words left her mouth. She saw the obvious hurt in his eyes. The comment seemed to hit harder than usual as though she had physically touched him in anger. *I'll handle him later. I don't have time now.* Gretchen turned on her heels and walked away determined to continue her search for the reporter and a killer. Finding Putnam was her main concern and would be the perfect cover for a little undercover work.

Chance felt as though he had been stung by a million bees. He shook his head and pinched the top of his nose with his thumb and finger. His head was hurting, and his heart was breaking.

"Lord, just let this night end with no casualties." He realized years ago that Gretchen could never be tamed, but he thought perhaps age had softened her independent streak. He had just been proven wrong.

Gretchen intently began her mission as she took one step toward the second floor of the house. She noticed the detective entering through the front doors, but she managed to sneak by him. As she took her first step, she realized she had been incorrect in her assumption.

"Ms. Malloy, exactly where are you going?"

She spun around but held her balance this time. *That man keeps me off-balance. He infuriates me! Kill him with kindness.* "Why, Detective Williams, I didn't see you there. I'm actually on an errand to find a missing reporter." Her voice was dripping in sweetness.

"Really? You've lost a reporter? Not you?" His voice dripped with sarcasm as he folded his arms in front of him, hopefully shielding him from any influence that woman held on him.

He seemed not to believe her. "I can't imagine why you would think I was lying to you. I would never do that. We should be trusting each other by now in our relationship." Gretchen fluttered her fake eyelashes. *Even though I know about your little fingerprinting and mugshot prank! But now is not the time. I have bigger fish to fry, but first I have to find him.*

It was best to ignore her comment, but he wanted to laugh out loud. Was he so transparent in finding her amusing and distracting? Williams eyed her up and down. He knew she was up to something. Whether it was really about a reporter, or some other fool's errand, Gretchen Malloy's little brain was working overtime. He thought he could hear it.

"Fine. Do whatever you are doing. But if you get in some kind of trouble, you need to yell."

"I never yell, Detective Williams. Well, there are few times in the throes of passion that I might actually scream out," Gretchen said as she threw back her hair seductively. Williams managed some control. He didn't like to be toyed with no matter how charming the player was. He responded with a glare. Gretchen gave up. "Fine, I'll make sure you know if I get in trouble. How's that?"

The man finally surrendered, walking away, muttering. "That woman will be the death of me and my career."

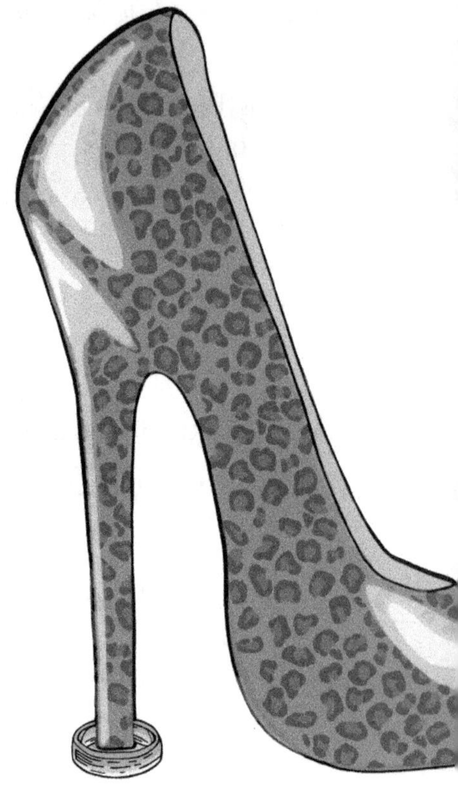

Chapter Thirteen

Gretchen quickly headed up the stairs. She thought she could smell the remnants of cigar smoke. Putnam's clothes always reeked of the stench. The reporter was a veritable chimney. She followed her nose. It smelled like a Cuban, and the fragrance led a trail toward the two double doors at the end of the hallway. *I know my cigars, and I always know the best of anything.* One of the doors was slightly ajar. She threw it open and saw the small statured reporter going through a book which looked like a diary Gretchen had when she was sixteen.

"What in the world are you doing, Putnam? Put that down."

Her voice startled him. His hands fumbled the book sending it falling onto the floor with several errant papers raining down onto the carpet.

"I was doing a little investigating."

Gretchen pointed out the door. "Leave now and I won't turn you in, but if you report on anything you found in that book, you are in some serious trouble. I won't offer you a story this time. I really will have the police arrest you. In fact, I figured you would do something like this, and I already have a detective at the ready to arrest you."

Putnam left the book and papers on the floor and scurried past Gretchen like a mouse caught in daylight.

From his position at the edge of the bedroom, he turned back. "Are they going to stay married? I mean, there's been rumors, and that little book proves the wife likes her young men. How is he going to run for a federal office with that baggage?"

Gretchen's eyes narrowed. She glared down at Putnam. With her heels, she was nearly a foot taller than the man. "Putnam, you need to go now before I lose my temper. You've seen it. Do you remember that time at the Junior League ball?" She saw the fear in his eyes. *That's the time I threatened to use a knife from the prime rib station.*

As she smiled, Gretchen placed her hands on his jacket lapels. He began to walk backward into the hallway as she came forward. "You will leave now, you little snake. You will not print one word. And don't think I won't call your boss on Monday. In fact, I'm having lunch with his wife next week." Putnam pushed away from the angry coordinator and fled the room before any of her threats came to fruition.

Gretchen shut the door soundly, content in her success. She would ruin the reporter if she had to in order to help Marty. As she faced the bedroom, she realized it was all hers to explore. *This was easy.*

She gathered up the book and the papers, placing them back on the desk. Gretchen tried not to look, but she could see that the papers were love letters. She pushed them farther away from her so she could read a few of the sentences. *It won't hurt to see what Putnam has seen, will it?* She turned a few pages over. Indeed, it was a diary of Olivia's lamentations.

The woman who had so much, seemed to feel as though she had nothing. She was in love with someone, or perhaps several someones, but not with her own husband.

"Martin is sweet, but he doesn't give me what I need. The others do, and I'm not ashamed to admit it if he asks," Gretchen read out loud. She shook her head. *Marty doesn't deserve this. No one deserved to not be loved.* She sighed for Marty and for herself. There was no time for self-pity, ever. *What other secrets does Olivia have? Now is my chance.*

Gretchen glanced around the room. It had to be the neatest bedroom of any one woman in the history of females. Not one item was out of place or pushed into a pile in any corner. By the bed, she searched in the nightstand's drawer. Even there, each item was in a neat little row. She sifted through a few more papers, jewelry, and a couple packages of condoms. Condoms? She grabbed one and placed it in her pocket. Maybe the police could match this with the one she had found?

Of course, Detective Debbie Downer had explained they couldn't use anything the intrepid amateur sleuth touched or found. She deemed his doubts ridiculous. *After all, I am a seasoned investigator.* Anything she found might help build a case. Besides, she knew most of the judges in Kansas City. They would give her the benefit of the doubt. *I'm only helping them. They should all understand that.*

Gretchen looked under the pillows. She looked under the bed and found a couple of pairs of shoes. Shoes. She headed for the closet. The area was as large as most bedrooms with separations between shoe shelves and clothing hangers. Placed in the middle of all of the shelves and cubbies was a mammoth island for more storage. *This could take me forever! Where would Olivia hide anything?* From the large double window on the west side, Gretchen could hear the music floating up from the patio. She quickly rifled through every cabinet within the island. They were filled with scarves and jewelry. Again, everything was in place.

"She can't be this organized all the time." Gretchen's frustration was getting the better of her, and she knew she had limited time until someone noticed she was missing from the event below. Gretchen's eyes were caught by a door ajar on the bathroom side of the room. That closet appeared as though it was overflowing with clothing thrown on the floor. It looked as though it was the one area that wasn't perfect in Olivia's world of fashion. Gretchen opened it, and several sweaters toppled on top of her head. She brushed her hair out of her eyes, and that's when she spotted a red-soled shoe poking from beneath a pair of jeans.

How could someone who has such an immaculate closet throw a pair of expensive stilettos at the bottom of such a trashy closet? Gretchen reached to pick up the shoe. She examined it. It was a good shoe, perhaps comfortable with the added inserts, but as she examined it closely she realized something important. Well, at least to her. Olivia's shoe was a knockoff, a good fake, but phony. *Where is the other one? Come on legs, don't fail me now.* Slowly dropping down on her knees, she began to feel around for another shoe. *Did Olivia really hide the evidence I need in a cluttered closet?*

She pushed back several other purses, and beneath a cheap knock-off of one of Gretchen's favorite designer's tote sat the other stiletto. Carefully, Gretchen lifted it out and saw what she thought she would. Not only did Olivia have secrets including fake footwear and knockoff bags, she had killer stilettos. Murderous stilettos. *This is dried blood on the heel, and I bet it was used on Trent.*

"That's not your shoe."

Olivia Stanton's voice stunned Gretchen into the gravity of the real situation she found herself in. *Lily will never allow me to forget this...if I live.* She wasn't Jessica Fletcher, nor was she Mata Hari. Even if she screamed, no one would hear her. Chance wouldn't come in on his white horse to rescue her. *I told him I didn't need him.* Detective Williams wouldn't be coming either. *He would probably hand Olivia the gun to kill me.* It seemed she had burned that bridge even though she thought they worked perfectly well as a team.

"Hand it to me now." Olivia's tone was guttural, frightening.

Gretchen crawled backward and placed her hand on the middle cabinet. She held tight to the shoe in her left while her right hand assisted in standing up. She was not going to lose this shoe. She backed away from Olivia.

"Gretchen, dear, give me that shoe. I've asked nicely. Don't make me use this." Olivia pulled a small gun from her pocket in the cocktail dress.

Stalling would be Gretchen's only option. *Maybe someone will realize Olivia and I are missing?* The band seemed to be playing louder. In fear and desperation, she backed up a few more steps until the window's ledge hit the top of her legs. She felt a hot breeze. The window was open. "You don't need to use that gun, besides, how will you explain shooting me?"

"I'll tell them I caught you stealing. Actually, I just knew you were too full of yourself. I was counting on you doing something stupid. You haven't disappointed me."

Gretchen needed an idea. *I haven't disappointed her? Well, she's the only one. What the hell am I going to do? I refuse to die at the hands of a nymphomaniac who has everything and wants more.* Fear blended with clarity. *Did I just describe myself? No. People will cry over my death, won't they? Lily will be a rich woman, and her children will be able to study at any college in the nation. Abby will love that gold and emerald ring I'm leaving her. But they won't have me. We have so many more bottles to drink and good meals to share. Gretchen, do something, old girl!*

Without taking her eyes off of the event planner, Olivia opened a drawer and pulled out a gold herringbone necklace. "I'll put this in your hand. Oh, and don't think I won't use this gun. Martin and I used to go shooting. I'm an excellent shot."

"No one will believe that I tried to steal that." Gretchen pointed at the necklace. "I own better."

"I can be very convincing."

Gretchen suddenly broke out into laughter. "Really? No one has believed a word you've said since you arrived in Kansas City. Oh sure, the club's members are impressed, but if you think they'll believe you over me, you're crazy. They understand that I know where everyone's skeletons are buried. Besides, I'm not a fake. They notice and recognize the genuine article, and you are not it. How do you think I've lasted this long? Recommendations, referrals, and rumors, honey. That's how it is done. Gretchen Malloy will always win out. My stilettos are the real thing, and so is my life."

"You are insane. You talk about yourself like you're something. You're nothing except annoying."

"Is that why you poisoned Trent? Because he was nothing? Why didn't you just shoot him?"

Olivia's loud laugh filled the room. Gretchen sat back on the ledge, nudging the window open farther with her backside. She still wasn't sure what she was going to do, but she at least wanted one option. She glanced down toward the patio. The cold buffet station was directly below the window. If she jumped, she would be impaled by an ice sculpture of the American flag. Shrimp surrounded it. She'd heard of swimming with the fishes, but cracking your head with the shrimp didn't really offer her an alternative to a gunshot.

"I didn't poison Trent, you idiot. You know nothing."

"I know you used this shoe to try to set me up." Gretchen waved the item in the air.

Olivia's low throaty laugh continued. "Oh, honey, I'm not trying. I've succeeded. After I shoot you for being the thief you are, they'll look through your things, and they'll find bottles of antidepressants and some love notes that Trent wrote to you."

"Why me?" Rather than the eyes of a raging madwoman, Gretchen saw sorrow in Olivia's.

"Because it was easy, just like you are. Martin had you on this pedestal, along with your dead little sister. I heard about you two every day. Amy used to say this, Gretchen did that. I got tired of it. Yes, he was sweet, but he has no ambition. He'd be happy being some defense attorney for indigent clients. I need this senatorial race to keep me sane. I married him for the money. You see, the IRS is beginning an investigation into my foundation. When I married Martin, my stocks were doing poorly. I panicked. Isn't it always about the money, Gretchen? It was the same with Trent. The boy became greedy. He sent me threatening notes when I couldn't sneak out. He thought he was in love."

Gretchen's eyes wandered over the entire closet. *Is there no way out of this? Get a grip. You aren't the mad woman in this room.* Olivia had paused in her explanation, looking down at the necklace in her hand.

"Then, when I explained to him that it was just sex, he decided to blackmail me. How dare he? Who did he think he was dealing with? I couldn't have that. Trent wasn't a necessary part of the equation, especially after I had his financials investigated. He had nothing, and his father had nearly nothing."

"Oh my God, and you think I'm self-absorbed! I have people who love me." Gretchen began to cry. Real tears actually flowed. She was speaking the truth. Her besties would miss her and her outrageous behavior. She hadn't even seen Lily's baby yet, and she was the fairy godmother. Gretchen Malloy, thankfully with water-proof mascara in place, was crying hysterically. *I'll show her a crazy woman!*

"But none of those people are here to save you, Ms. Malloy." Behind Olivia stood Marty's campaign manager, Ryan. For a brief second, Gretchen thought she was saved until he kissed Olivia on the cheek. *I knew it! They are in this together and all those looks they gave each other did mean exactly what I thought they meant! Ha!* Yet, getting something right never felt so awful. *He won't fall for my tears. I'll have to try something else. Think, and think very quickly. This room is filled with killers.*

"Darling, you go down to the party. I'll take care of this like I take care of every crisis or problem. This one will be easy to dispose of properly."

Olivia didn't budge. "I'm staying. I can't wait for her to get what she deserves."

Gretchen breathed in deeply and stopped crying. She knew what she needed to do now. She needed to know everything, to stall. "So, it wasn't Olivia's son who poisoned Trent, and Marty wasn't sent a suspicious package from some lunatic? Well he was, but it was from his lunatic wife and campaign manager. It wasn't Olivia's son who went to see Trent. You look so much like him. I see that now. You were friends with him too, weren't you?"

"Yes, we knew each other when we were kids. Later, we all met up in college. Trent was one of my fraternity brothers. The week of the wedding, Trent was easily accessible. After he began to push Olivia, I made sure I became friendly with him again. I showed up at the tennis courts and at his favorite bar. He didn't think anything of me bringing a flask of his favorite bourbon to toast him on his wedding day. By then, he knew there wasn't going to be a wedding."

"And you separated him from his groomsmen with the flat tire. Right, Ryan?" Gretchen lifted her chin in full impudent fashion. *I'll pretend I'm in charge. I've always been a great actress. Always.*

Ryan smirked. "It was easy enough. The vehicle was parked outside of his home. I just took my utility knife and punctured away. Ms. Malloy, you of all people should realize that no one is paying attention to anyone but the bridal party on a wedding day."

"You're wrong, Ryan. I pay attention to everything at every wedding and every event. To be the best, you can't be sloppy. You must be perfect each and every time. I knew you were involved." Gretchen's haughtiness wasn't playing well with the two murderers. "Trent needed a ride, and no one went with him to the church. No one would've thought anything of a helpful ride from a friend's mother. The boy may have been a lot of things, but he was punctual."

"Especially when he knew he was going to receive a rather large paycheck to marry Leslie. I drove him so he could think," Olivia said calmly. "That little bride waltzed in and jeopardized everything. Trent and I had one final fling. We had a little champagne, and a little, well that's not important. She announced to him that she was stopping the wedding. After she left, I came out from my hiding place, and he told me we can be together because he never intended on marrying her. He was going to embarrass his parents when he arrived at the altar. He had some check and a prenup in his pocket. He was going to rip them up and walk out. He was blackmailing me because he loved me and wanted to be with me. What an idiot! The bride's dad gave him a quarter of a million dollars."

Ryan gave Olivia a quick peck on the cheek. "You see, Ms. Malloy, I didn't mind sharing Olivia, but Trent needed to know his place. He kept pushing. He wanted her all to himself, and that was not acceptable. We offered him a place in our little arrangement, but that was disgusting to him. I knew what I needed to do."

Gretchen wiped away a tear and tried to calm her tapping foot. "So you don't mind sharing Olivia? That's obvious since Marty is the one who is married to her."

"Martin is a good man," Olivia cried out. "He didn't think a thing about Ryan and me spending so much time together. In fact, Martin was thrilled that we got along so well, and that Ryan was a friend of my sons. Besides, what my husband doesn't know won't hurt him, and there's no way anyone will convince him that I was involved in a murder. He doesn't suspect anything except my indiscretion with Trent, thanks to the police. But, I'll smooth it over. You could say Martin is clueless."

Gretchen continued to stall. *This is silly! Where is Chance or Detective Williams? Shouldn't they miss me by now? Maybe I could tap in Morse code on the floor with my heel? They won't hear me in this house. And I don't know Morse code.* "You really don't mind sharing Olivia with Marty?"

Ryan and Olivia laughed. "Of course not. He serves a purpose, doesn't he, darling?" Ryan turned to Olivia and kissed her tenderly on the cheek.

"Gretchen, Marty is a lovely man, but I just need more," Olivia admitted. "Ryan knows his place, and he does anything I ask him to do, but Trent wouldn't be a good boy."

It was all coming together in Gretchen's mind. "Olivia, you didn't poison him, did you?"

"No, I didn't know about that. I figured we would scare him, but if it had to be that way then so be it. I didn't know what Ryan had done."

"But," Gretchen interrupted, "someone put antidepressants in the champagne or in the flutes. Why didn't you pass out?"

Ryan chuckled. "Don't you think I know what Olivia can handle? She takes those pills quite frequently. I dropped enough in that champagne to at least knock him out. He didn't think anything of Olivia arriving with an open bottle to celebrate. Besides, I remembered when Trent was ill as a child. I just confirmed it when we all were out one night. In college, he had to watch how much he drank, but when he did overdo it, he became so ill one night he was rushed to the hospital. He shouldn't have been drinking as much as he was. That last week before the wedding, I made sure we reclaimed our frat boy reputations. We closed bars all over town and consumed gallons of alcohol. Olivia's sons were oblivious that they were assisting in the murder of their friend. When I gave him the flask for one final celebratory drink on the wedding day, I hoped the bourbon on top of what he'd already consumed would do him in. Oh that, and I made sure he couldn't breathe."

Gretchen nodded. "The peanut oil? What did you do, rim the champagne glasses?"

Ryan smiled widely. "Give that woman a stuffed elephant. You are a winner, Ms. Malloy, but not for long. Trent didn't go down that easy. I had to place my hand over his mouth. That did the trick quickly."

"What? You suffocated him?" Gretchen wondered if Detective Williams knew that Trent had been smothered, or choked, or whatever. Suddenly, she was feeling sick. Stoic Gretchen, a tower of calm, was becoming a muddled puddle of fear and queasiness. Thankfully, she wasn't standing on her high heels. *Think, Gretchen. You can't stall much longer. No wonder those crime dramas have the killer or victim talking so much. Time. I need time.*

Olivia noticed the change in Gretchen. "Honey, you don't look like you're feeling very well. You have no way out. It's over. We've found the murderer, and she came up to my closet to steal and to frame me. Everyone will know that Gretchen really wanted Martin and couldn't stand the fact that I have him. In more than one way, you're trapped, Ms. Malloy. Now, give me that shoe. It's over." The gun was pointing directly at the victim, not the murderer.

"Oh, it's over," Gretchen murmured. *What can I do? I'll play my strongest hand.* Gretchen sat up straighter, thrusting her chest forward while lifting her chin as high as possible. She crossed her legs and dangled one leg over the other confidently. *I'll do what I do best. I'll exude confidence, and I'll annoy the hell out of them before I die.*

"Ryan, don't you think it was a little overkill? Seriously, you had all your bases covered from the liquor, to the antidepressants, and the peanut oil. Then, to suffocate the poor boy, that was a bit much. He must've struggled quite a bit when his medical bracelet went flying. You were very messy." Gretchen looked down as though she was disappointed in his performance. "You are so young and have so much to learn."

Ryan lurched forward in defiance; his hands placed on the island in front of him. "I didn't have to struggle with him. I don't know what you're talking about."

Gretchen watched as Olivia lowered the gun. The woman touched the young man. "Ryan, I pulled it off of him."

Ryan eyes questioned Olivia's. "Did he hurt you? Was he hurting you? If he was, then I'm even happier that he is gone. He was worthless."

Gretchen noticed Olivia's nervousness. The woman balanced on one foot and then the other. She sported puppy dog eyes, looking up at Ryan for some sort of forgiveness. *I think my light bulb just turned on!*

"Trent didn't hurt her," Gretchen commented coldly. "She and he had one final, well let's use the word reunion. The bracelet must've broken in the throes of passion. Is that what happened, Olivia?" Gretchen fluttered her eyelashes. Ryan looked at Olivia and then Gretchen. That's when the coordinator added one more detail in her developing plan. "Olivia, you know that the police realize the lipstick on the glass was yours, but what you haven't been told is they also have the condom you used. You know, the one with your lipstick on it when you had your mouth--"

Ryan pushed Olivia's hand away from his arm. "You said you were done with him when he threatened you. You were just supposed to share a drink with him, sedate him, scare him. I was the one who decided he should be finished off. You just couldn't help yourself! Someone could've seen you two, but you had to feed your needs? I was okay with sharing you, but your carelessness is too dangerous for my future. Now, you'll lose me too. You disgust me."

"Ryan," Olivia yelled. "She's trying to pull us apart. She's lying. I do care about you and your future, our future."

Gretchen watched in hope as Olivia placed the gun onto the island.

"I may be many things, but I'm not a liar. You know that, Ryan. You and I are professionals. I can't afford to be seen as a dishonest person. I found the condom in the dumpster. That nice Detective Williams has it. He knows."

He'd be nicer if he broke into this room like a cowboy storming a saloon after a long dry cattle drive. "And they'll have this shoe. There's no way out for you." Gretchen steadied herself on the windowsill.

Olivia pushed back tears and picked up the gun, aiming directly at her foe. "Throw the shoe onto the counter. Now, Gretchen. I swear I'll shoot you."

"You can't have this shoe," Gretchen said calmly even though her insides were burning. She dropped the footwear out into the night air with no way of knowing where it landed. *They don't have it.*

Gretchen moved away from the window as one shot was fired. She crouched behind the cabinet and grabbed her head, waiting for imminent death. She heard a scuffle as Ryan reprimanded Olivia for firing.

"You stupid woman. Someone is going to hear that."

Gretchen heard another shot as someone broke down the locked bedroom door. She heard a fight. She peaked around to see Detective Williams grab the gun from Olivia and pistol whip young Ryan to the floor.

Surprisingly, he smiled at her. "Ms. Malloy, you can come out now."

Gretchen slowly rose from her hiding place. She smoothed her hair and dress. "Wow, we are a great team."

"We are not a team." He busily phoned for backup. "I want some explanation for all of this, whatever all of this is. Put your hands up, Ms. Malloy."

"What?" Gretchen's mouth gaped open. "They were trying to kill me."

"She was stealing, and I think she killed that poor groom. She was attempting to frame me. She had these shoes she was putting in my closet, and she said she had enough drugs on her tonight to kill Martin and me." Olivia's crocodile tears flowed freely, her lips pouted as if she were a spoiled pathetic child. She collapsed on the bed in a heap. Ryan remained sprawled on the carpet.

"Detective, you know that isn't true." Gretchen still had not put her arms up and was coming closer to Williams.

"That's far enough," he instructed. "I don't know anything, Ms. Malloy."

Gretchen was hurt. *How dare he!* "You know me. We've worked together on this thing. We've been growing, side by side, into a great team of investigators."

Williams shook his head. "Yeah, kind of like mold growing, or moss taking over a tree until it chokes it. Get those hands up."

Gretchen wanted to place her hands on her hips and stomp away, but that didn't seem to be an option. Instead, she gave up and did as he commanded. At least she didn't have a gun pointed at her, yet. *At least the bad guys don't have the gun, and Williams will have far too much paperwork if he shoots me.*

As Ryan stirred, he held his head and sat up slowly. He motioned for Williams.

"I was worried about the future senator's safety since we arrived here, but my concern was with Ms. Malloy. She's the one who has sent those threats and that suspicious package." Ryan's voice trembled as he lied.

"Oh for the love of martinis, football, and expensive lipstick," Gretchen wailed. "They are both lying, Detective Williams."

"That's another thing. Olivia did have an affair with Trent Hampton, but Gretchen stole Olivia's lipstick," Ryan added. "I saw her stick it in her bag. She stole some of Mrs. Stanton's pills. She was going to drug us. We were in fear for our lives."

Gretchen rolled her eyes and lowered her arms despite the detective's threats. "Oh for heaven's sake. My arms are getting tired, and this is getting ridiculous. I mean, really, would I wear that shade of pink? Of course not. That's not my look. Besides, it is just too young for a woman of my maturity." Gretchen's brows furrowed in confusion. *Did I just admit I'm old?* "My style is definitely not pink, and I don't have any of that stuff. Besides, I've never taken any medication more powerful than an aspirin." Gretchen looked directly into Williams' beautiful eyes. "And the only thing I've ever stolen has been a kiss." She stomped with her left foot in anger and found an ottoman close to the door. "If you need me, I'll be sitting over here."

Two more detectives entered the room, along with police officers, and Chance. In their hands were all of Gretchen's bags. Her interest peaked as she saw evidence bags holding several pill bottles, a pink lipstick, and a silver-colored flask.

"Well, Mr. Alexander?" Williams asked as Chance threw all the items on a sideboard counter.

"They were all in Ms. Malloy's bags."

Gretchen began to protest and decided to finally take her attorney's advice from weeks ago. *I'm going to keep my mouth shut.*

"Officers, arrest Mrs. Stanton and Mr. Marley here." Williams pointed his gun in their direction despite their moaning and loud accusations.

Once Olivia and Ryan were in handcuffs, Detective Williams holstered his firearm and passed Olivia's gun to one of his detectives. Chance offered a comforting smile in Gretchen's direction. He knew something she didn't.

Gretchen forced a smile. "You two men are absolutely worthless. Detective Williams, Chance, you are both smart men. You need to use your brains."

Chance shook his head. "We have. You see, what you and these two don't know was that the detective, and I have been doing our own bit of investigating. Olivia, Marty gave me permission to tap all of the phones after he learned of your indiscretion. He also gave me access to the security video on the property, to look in every room, including your bedroom when Marty was away. I'm not sure what you see in Ryan here, but--" Chance's explanation sent Olivia into a rage.

"How dare you!"

"Because I asked him to," Detective Williams answered. "Mr. Stanton was more than willing to assist in the investigation. He'd already authorized Chance to do all that was needed to upgrade security at the house. He had no problem turning over the footage to us. The cameras were up and running today, catching you in the act." He turned to Gretchen. For one of the only times in her life she sat passively in the corner. "Ms. Malloy really had been uncovering some remarkable evidence. When a match is struck, there is eventually a fire. It looks like you folks were caught in your own flash fire."

"But, she had all of that in her bags. Why aren't you arresting her?" Ryan demanded.

"Because, I checked every bag that came into this house," Chance answered. "I did a thorough search of Gretchen's things early in the day. One of my men was with me while I did it. We even searched her car. None of these items were anywhere in her possession or even near her. We also have the security footage from that room. I watched in real time as Ryan placed those items in Ms. Malloy's bags. I also followed him when he informed Mrs. Stanton that the job had been done."

"Yes," Gretchen yelled out loud. *I knew it! They had that little meeting by the pool.*

Williams smiled. "She is correct on a few other things too. She would never wear that shade of pink. And one thing about Ms. Malloy, she is authentic, the real deal from her lips to her feet. She'd never wear the cheap stuff you've been passing off as designer, Mrs. Stanton."

Gretchen perked up, her lips fashioning a smile at her detective. "You do know me. That's the nicest thing anyone has ever said about me."

"Don't get used to it," Williams responded. "Oh, and I'm sure when we check the shoe we will find it has Trent Hamptons' blood on it. We will be able to get enough off of it to make a match. So folks, it is over."

"It certainly is." Martin Stanton's voice boomed throughout the room as he entered. He paused, standing between Chance and Gretchen. "Olivia, Ryan, both of you are on your own. I'm done with you."

Gretchen saw the despondency in his eyes. The poor man had been through so much to find love. As his wife and campaign manager were taken away, surrounded by police, he turned away and shook Chance's hand.

"I can't thank you enough, Chance."

Chance shook his head and pointed toward the only woman remaining in the room. "Thank Gretchen. She's the one who kept following all the leads no matter what. Through all of this, she's always been concerned about you."

Marty came over to her and pulled her up from her seat. He brought her into his arms and sobbed. "Now what? It's all over. My happiness, my love, the race--"

Gretchen patted him as though he was the little brother she had never had. "It will get better. You know that. Remember, God only gives you as much as He and you can handle."

Chance and Williams chuckled. Gretchen bobbed her head up from the embrace. "What? I believe in God. I'm attempting to have a moment here." *Those two shouldn't be allowed to become friends.*

Marty kissed her on the cheek and pulled away. Tears left streams down his cheeks, but he began to laugh. "Only you, dear Gretchen would plan at this exact moment to quote inspirational advice to a man who has just lost everything."

The other two men shared the laugh, but Gretchen raised a finger to silence them to mild chuckling. "Marty Stanton, you have not lost everything. You have money, your health, and you still have friends like me who will stand by you no matter what. I am nothing but loyal."

"And one Gretchen equals hundreds, Marty," Chance added.

Williams' brows furrowed. "And one Gretchen is certainly enough. I can honestly admit I've never met anyone quite like you."

Gretchen curtsied. "No, you haven't, nor will you ever. I am one of a kind! Gentlemen, I'm going to take everything you are saying as complimentary. By the way, Chance Alexander, I'm not sure I like you placing your hands on all of my things. I had intimate garments in those bags."

One of Chance's brows arched. "Really? You're upset because I touched your extra pair of panties? I've touched more than that."

Williams turned so she wouldn't see him laughing. *I'll ignore both of them. I don't have time to banter with a couple of children. I have a job to do.* She grabbed Marty by the arm and pushed him near the bedroom entrance. She stopped next to the detective. "When you contain yourself, you need to get that shoe. Where did it land?"

"You did manage to miss the shrimp. My officers have it. It ended up perched on top of the flag."

"Ah, good. Oh, and if you get a chance to question Olivia, ask her why she used those stilettos on that boy's neck. I know she was trying to frame me, but I'm completely offended that she used a pair of knockoffs. I only wear the real things, or I go barefoot. Now, Marty, come on. You are running for the United States Senate."

"Gretchen, no, I can't. Not now," he protested as she pulled him along as though he was a child being led off to his first day in school.

"Marty Stanton, you are a good man who has overcome too much to slink into a corner just because your wife is a sociopathic nymphomaniac. Now come on. I'll be your manager until you can find someone more suitable. Of course, I could do it. I flatter myself that I can take on anything. Did I tell you the time that the President flew into Kansas City, and he wanted me to--"

As her voice trailed off, Chance and Williams collected a few other items in the room, including the diary. Other officers were instructed to do a thorough search. "Marty has to go through with it. She won't allow him not to," Chance remarked.

"Does she ever take no for an answer?" Williams' question stopped Chance in his tracks.

"Usually never. Years ago, she told me no, and I told her no. I've regretted that day all my life. Don't let her say no again, and always say yes to her. Most days, that's the only way you'll get her to shut up. Besides, she's worth the insanity, the headaches, and even the ear plugs."

Williams stopped. "Ear plugs?"

Chance smiled. "Yep. Ear plugs. Trust me."

The two men looked at each other with some silent form of understanding.

"So, what you're saying is never tell her no?" Williams was searching for some kind of an answer when it came to Gretchen Malloy.

Chance's lips formed a slim knowing smile. "I'm saying she'll never accept it again."

Williams understood. "Ah. Got it. Gretchen, just say yes."

As if on cue, Gretchen ran back into the room, grabbing the detective's hand, and placing a small object into it. His eyes widened when he recognized what it was. "What the heck?"

"Detective, it is a condom." She shook her head and looked up to the ceiling. "I know you've seen one before. Well, I found it here in the room, and I'm sure if you can match things like that, you'll discover it is the same brand as the one we found in the glass."

"We're completing a sweep of the room, but I can't use this. There's no chain of evidence. You've been warned about that on numerous occasions."

She seemed irritated beyond reason. "Fine. I know. I have to help Marty, but I'm sure you can figure out something to do with it. Use it, for all I care."

She raced off, her heels clicking on the wood floors.

Williams shook his head in disbelief. Chance bent over in laughter. "What was that?"

Chance caught his breath and patted the other man on the back. "That was Gretchen, and that's why you can't tell her no."

"But she wants me to use this?" He waved the item in the air.

Chance roared with laughter. "Safety first, Detective Williams?"

Chapter Fourteen

"Marty, it doesn't look that bad. Look at this article. They are impressed with your education program." Gretchen spread the newspaper across the table. "Do you want some more coffee?" She headed over to the breakfast bar by the pool before her friend answered.

"It helps that you blackmailed that Putnam fellow for a two-night interview on his station's prime broadcast," Marty remarked blandly. He was beginning to think that he might have a chance, and it did help that Gretchen was his main cheerleader. He didn't want to allow too much hope. He was beginning to feel like himself again. In another month, the chaos would simmer down as the story died. He would begin traveling the state soon, alone.

"Putnam owed me, besides he knows a good thing when he sees it." She embraced Marty's shoulders as she leaned over him. "And you are a good man, Marty Stanton. Don't you ever forget it."

"And you are a loyal friend, Gretchen Malloy."

Gretchen looked up to see Chance coming toward the patio. His garment bag was slung over his shoulder, and he was rolling a piece of luggage behind him.

"She's a good woman, that's for sure," he said, flashing a knowing smile.

"You're ready to leave me for a bit?" Marty asked the

question, but Gretchen wanted to know the same thing.

"Just a little while. I'll be back in September for your main push and that bus tour of the state you have planned. Of course, I'll be there in November when you win." Chance winked at Gretchen.

"I don't know about that, Chance. I got into this late, and now with all the controversy, winning could just be a pipe dream."

Gretchen patted his back. "Look, Marty, you need to be confident. Think of it this way. They'll never forget you with all this media splash."

Chance shook his head. She always could transform something bad into good. "Listen to the lady, Marty. She won't fail you." Chance looked into her eyes. The woman's eyes could bore a hole in your soul. The day she said she wouldn't follow him, he retaliated telling her he wouldn't change his mind. He had failed her and hadn't considered her for one minute. He thought she'd follow him. Those eyes turned cold. But he saw a warmth toward him now. She wasn't wearing those tarantula-long fake eyelashes, but she had enough mascara on to scare a racoon. She looked like his G. Always his G.

Gretchen came over to Chance's side. "Let me take you to the airport."

"I have one of my guys driving me."

"I'll deny I ever said this, but please let me take you." Her plea hit his heart and struck its mark.

He didn't want to end this visit with her in an argument. He nodded. Gretchen clapped with happiness. "Besides, I really need to take a break from Marty," she whispered. "I don't need to be hovering over him like a mother hen."

"That's good of you," Chance whispered in response. "A little Marty goes a long way."

She sighed. "That's for sure. Now, come on. Let's get you to that baby." She kissed Marty and assured him she would return the next day.

On the way to the airport, the conversation was light, and there was not one word about Olivia or the murder.

"Does your daughter know the sex of the baby yet?"

"No, but I'm hoping for a girl."

"Chance Alexander, I thought you wanted a boy? You wanted all that male bonding. I don't believe you." Chance had been a star football player. *He'll want to teach a grandson everything he knows about the sport.*

"Nah, I like little girls. Heck, I like big girls too."

Gretchen giggled. "Yes, you do. I think you have become more charming than you were when we were in college. If that is even possible."

He rubbed her shoulder as she drove. "You think I'm charming?"

"You always were, but I believe in maturity you have this certain flair."

"My, my, that's a compliment coming from the queen of flair. By the way, I'm glad you dropped the fake lashes."

"Oh, I only wear them when I might see someone. I will never be without them at a wedding or an event. If I'm in front of a camera they are required accessories."

"I get it. Heavy mascara is for your relaxed days."

"When I won't be seeing anyone."

Chance acted as though he had been shot in the chest. "You wound me, woman. I'm not anyone."

Suddenly, Gretchen's smile vanished. "You are everything," she whispered.

An uncomfortable silence filled the car until they pulled into the airport's drive. "Gretchen, I will be back. This time I'm not letting you off the hook that easily."

"There's a parking spot. I'll drop you by the door." Gretchen heard him, but she didn't want or know how to answer him. He had been the one who went into the Marines. He was the one who had left her behind because she had other dreams. She was the one who didn't want to follow behind.

She parked quickly. Chance jumped out, grabbing his two bags, and his laptop. She came around to the back of the car. He stood there like a lost puppy.

"Chance--"

He shook his head. "Don't say anything you don't mean, G. You know I love you, and I will be back. I'll take my chances that you'll still be here."

Gretchen stood inches away from him. "You know I'll be here, silly. Do you think someone is going to swoop in and snatch me up?"

"Seriously, I do. It'll be some good man who believes in you. He'll have to be strong to be with you, and he'll always have to say yes to you." He winked at her.

"Kiss me, Chance."

Chance dropped his bags dramatically with a heavy thud on the ground. He kept his laptop in his hand as he folded her into his arms. The kiss was magnificent, reigniting the fire that had always burned between them. Gretchen was breathless when she pulled back.

"I want you to know this before you go," Gretchen said as he picked up his bags. "I have always loved you, and that will never change. When I told you I didn't need you or anyone, that doesn't mean I don't want you. You come back to me, even for a little while. I can live with that. You'll have your life, and I'll have mine. It's who we are."

"I'll be back." Chance turned to walk away. "I'll call you when I get to Virginia."

Gretchen's heart was breaking. She could only nod. She composed herself and threw back her hair. "Just text. I will probably be very busy later tonight with some gorgeous man. After all, I am Gretchen Malloy!"

"Yes, you are. I'll text. I sure don't want to interrupt you and your new friend. See you when I come back, G."

He walked into the terminal and vanished. Gretchen drove away. On the interstate, she brushed back a few tears and wiped away her sniffles. *Will he come back? Will we become a couple with an open, long distance romance? Will that be enough for him? Will that be enough for me?*

Even though she had been involved in a murder, Gretchen was in demand now more than ever. She had several new clients who wanted her just because of the notoriety. She didn't mind that. Any publicity, even the bad was good publicity. She would ride this wave of fame as long as she could. As she drove home alone, she went over her schedule in her thoughts. She planned on taking the rest of the week off to do absolutely nothing and to bolster Marty's ego. Soon, she would be back planning events and weddings. *Thank God!*

She decided to use the valet parking service at the apartment and pulled the car into the front driveway. One of the young men came to her side, opening her door as he greeted her. "You have a visitor, Ms. Malloy."

"I do? That's an unexpected surprise."

Indeed it was a surprise as she came around her vehicle to see Detective Williams waiting for her. He was smiling. *Now, what did I do? Are they accusing me of some other crime?* An otter escaped the zoo the other night. She had nothing to do with its disappearance. She wasn't into otters. *Chinchillas are another story.*

"This is a surprise, Detective Williams." Gretchen smiled sweetly as she neared him. "Have you come to admit in person that I make you a better detective?"

"It's Daniel, by the way." He completely ignored her comment.

"Really?" *I really want to laugh my head off, but that would be so rude. The poor man. His mother must've loved the actor or the character.*

"I know. That's why I go by Daniel and not Danny like in that old television show."

Gretchen pushed past him into the building's foyer. He followed.

"Have I done something again?"

The detective shifted back and forth a bit. "Well no, but yes, but no."

Gretchen eyed him suspiciously. She examined him closely. *He doesn't have a tie or jacket on, and I don't see a gun. I'm not sure where he could hide it.* He was wearing jeans with a short-sleeved polo. His hair was a little mussed, his face unshaven. His tanned, muscled arms rivaled the beauty of his eyes. *He's so, so cute.*

"Maybe I shouldn't have come. There's no football to watch. I haven't brought you a martini, and I absolutely couldn't tell the difference between a cheap or expensive lipstick without looking at the pricetag," Williams murmured. He turned to go, and Gretchen grasped his hand.

"Have you come just to visit me?" Apparently, any wall of pretense was felled in that one handholding. *It feels like a current is running through my body. Is this possible? Chance and I have this same energy, and now...*

"I've come to apologize for something I've done." His voice was soft, softer than it had ever been in the course of the murder investigation.

Gretchen didn't let go of his hand. She liked this voice. She liked his uncertainty. *I like him.*

"You want to make amends for the fingerprint ink that took a week of scrubbing to remove? Or do we want to discuss how that mugshot photo should be destroyed?"

Williams lowered his gaze to his feet and nodded. Slowly, he lifted his head and peered directly into her eyes, her very pretty eyes. It was as though he was seeing the real her for the first time. "I'm sorry for that. It made me feel better at the time. I used the mugshot for target practice, and I did destroy the negative. Forgive me."

"Well, thank you for the apology. I wondered when you would get around to saying something, or if you would."

Williams noticed that she still held his hand. "I owe you. Maybe sometime we could go for drinks or for coffee? A friend of mine owns a lovely place. He makes his own pastries."

Gretchen tightened her hold on his hand. "Do you have time now? Do you want to come up, maybe order some takeout? I'll make martinis, we can watch my film of the Chiefs' Super Bowl win, and if we have time, I'll teach you all about expensive lipstick."

His bashful behavior faded as he studied her closely. She wasn't wearing those fake lashes. Her red lipstick was absent from her lips. There was just something about her that you couldn't forget, and it wasn't just the incessant clicking of those blasted stiletto heels. A wise man had told him never to tell her no. For some irrational, brain-twisting reason, he didn't want to today.

"Gretchen, yes, I would like that very much." They stood shoulder-to-shoulder in the elevator, still holding each other's hand.

Notes From the Author

Gretchen Malloy was first mentioned in The Poppy Drop, A Lily List Mystery. The wedding and event coordinator and planner was feared and at times, despised by wedding florist Lily Schmidt and her assistant Abby. Gretchen and her over-the-top personality became a fan favorite in the second adventure The Hibiscus Heist. The noise of tapping fingernails on a car window and clicking heels on a floor became her signature.

Women like Gretchen live in every community. I bet you have met one or two in your life. Here in Kansas City, they frequent society weddings and dress for Sunday brunch at the best restaurants. They are women who have every hair in place, and their personality is just as powerful as their wardrobe. We are grateful for their charity work, and the valuable jobs they perform in every level of our workforce.

I just never got the hang of wearing stilettos. I've tried them on. I've fallen over. I've worn high heels, but stilettos need just the right leg and slender foot. And to wear them well, you need to be someone like Gretchen Malloy!

Watch for Gretchen's second story soon! She'll be meeting up with a main character from The Lily List Mysteries. Our intrepid amateur sleuth runs into more trouble, a little romance, intrigue, and of course, she does it all with her heels on!

Contact C.L. Bauer at clbauerkc@gmail.com and sign up for promotions, contests, and news at www.clbauer. com. Free chapters are available when you sign up for the monthly newsletter.

C.L. BAUER

C.L. Bauer grew up and lives in Kansas City, Missouri. Her first novel The Poppy Drop, A Lily List Mystery was well received by the top 100 Books of Independent Publishers when it launched in 2018.

The Lily List Mystery Series features the highly organized, post-it note, and list making florist Lily Schmidt. Readers have enjoyed the adventures of the mystery loving woman and the wedding stories that are highlighted in these novels. Ms. Bauer draws on true events from her family's wedding and event flower business. With over one hundred years of serving families on their special days, Clara's Flowers has received numerous awards in the wedding world, including "best of" and "legacy winner" for service and design.

C.L. Bauer's first love of writing provided an early career in journalism. During high school, she began as a sports reporter, became an editor in college, and continued professionally in every writing medium including advertising and creative direction.

The author enjoys her family, travel, a good book on a rainy day, bulk post-it notes, and meeting her readers. She can always be swayed to feast on Mexican food, watch a hockey game, and drink the occasional fruity libation. If you've read her novels, you already know she loves Kansas City during the holidays.

You can reach C.L. Bauer on all forms of social media including her author pages on Facebook, Instagram, Twitter, Amazon, and Goodreads. Please review this and any of C.L. Bauer's published works. They are widely available for purchase in print and e-book forms. She's available for book club discussions virtually or in-person.

As always, happy reading!

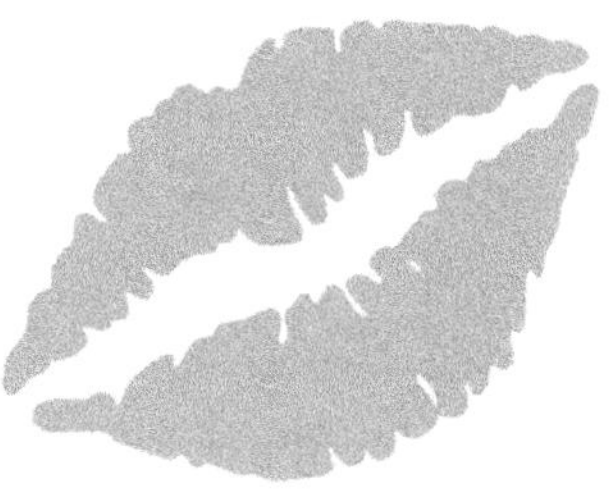

Sign up at www.clbauer.com for this author's newsletter, promotions, pre-order information, free chapters, and upcoming publications. Contact C.L. Bauer directly at clbauerkc@gmail.com.

This is the first Exclusive of The Lily List Mystery Series. Each Exclusive features more adventures with Lily's friends. Mysteries, murders, and more romance are coming your way!